Tales of
Turtle River

TALES OF
TURTLE RIVER

Sherry Williams
illustrations by Grant Williams

To Pat,

My neighbor and traveling companion.
I hope you enjoy!
Sherry

iUniverse, Inc.
New York Lincoln Shanghai

Tales of Turtle River

iUniverse books may be ordered through booksellers or by contacting:

iUniverse
2021 Pine Lake Road, Suite 100
Lincoln, NE 68512
www.iuniverse.com
1-800-Authors (1-800-288-4677)

This book is a work of fiction inspired by stories my father told of his life growing up in Jupiter, Florida in the 1920's. Some characters are based on real people he told me about, and other characters come totally from my imagination.

ISBN-13: 978-0-595-36049-9 (pbk)
ISBN-13: 978-0-595-80500-6 (ebk)
ISBN-10: 0-595-36049-1 (pbk)
ISBN-10: 0-595-80500-0 (ebk)

Printed in the United States of America

This book is dedicated to the memory of the real life Fritz, with gratitude to my husband and illustrator, Grant, and gratitude to my writing groups and to the many people who helped and encouraged me in getting this book published.

CONTENTS

▼

I sat alone in my car watching from across the street. The house that held my childhood within its walls, the brown shingled, two story house beside the Turtle River, was about to come down. Oh, I hadn't been in it for seventy years, but at that moment I could feel the ghosts of my past reaching out to me.

There was Mama, in her checked cotton dress, her auburn hair pulled into a knot on top of her head. She was walking toward the river with my youngest brother and sister, two dark haired tykes running ahead of her carrying fishing poles. All seven of us, the Vicelli kids, resembled our Italian born daddy, not our fair Irish blue-eyed mama.

A screen door banged, and I saw myself come out into the yard.

That vision in my mind faded and one particular day came forward. It was the day Charles Lindbergh made his first, lonely flight across the Atlantic.

MAY 21, 1927

Baseball was on my mind. I was a barefoot, skinny twelve-year-old with a mop of sun-streaked hair and ears that stuck out a bit too far.

I pedaled my bike to Partridge Farms, hoping to catch a ball game in the field. Mr. Partridge was standing beside the milk house talking to Old Man Hansen when I wheeled into the yard. He waved his hat to me and called, "Hey Fritz! Did you hear about Lindbergh?"

"No, Sir. Did he land?"

"In Paris! Just came over the radio a few minutes ago." Mr. Partridge smiled and shook his head. "The Spirit of St. Louis. What's next?"

Old Man Hansen contorted his white whiskered face and spat out a wad of chewing tobacco. "Rubbish," he said. "If we was meant to fly all over the world like that, the Lord 'ave given us wings."

"Shoot, J.M., get your head out of the sand, this is the 20th Century," said Mr. Partridge. "Renato was here earlier," he said, looking at me, "but he and the rest of the gang took off in the truck for town."

"Aw, that's okay Mr. Partridge," I said, looking at the ground to hide my disappointment. Town was West Palm Beach, a good hour's drive. Renato, my brother, was four years older than I and seemed to be forever going off without me.

A loud mooing came from the milk house. Mr. Partridge laughed. "Talk with you later, J.M. You too, Fritz. Got some girls waiting for me." He winked and ducked in the door.

After that, Old Man Hansen signaled me over to his pick-up truck. "Looky what I got here, son."

In the back of his rusted black truck was a box, and inside, snuggled together, were two sleeping puppies.

"Those Lady's puppies, Mr. Hansen?"

"Sure 'nough. Pure redbone hounds. Both male. Goin' to grow to be a couple of fine huntin' dogs."

I reached down and stroked one. It yawned and stretched, then opened its eyes and looked at me. I picked up the little fellow, snuggled its warm fuzzy body against my face and took in its puppy smell. "Sure is cute, Mr. Hansen."

"Them's the last of the litter." He took more tobacco from his pouch and eyed me, like he could read my mind. "Sixty dollars fer the two of 'um."

I poked my hand into my shorts pocket. Sixty dollars! I knew I didn't have that kind of money. But my fingers hit upon something. Daddy's watch. I just happened to notice it lying on the counter of the china cabinet when I was leaving the house. Mama always wants us to be on time for supper, so I figured I'd borrow it so I'd know what time to head home. Don't know what I was thinking when my fingers found it in my pocket, but before I realized what I was doing, I was dangling Daddy's gold pocket watch from its chain in front of Mr. Hansen and asking him if he'd take a trade.

Old Man Hansen smiled a near toothless smile. "Them's valuable pups. Don't come cheap, Sonny."

He examined the watch, shaking his head back and forth. "How about one pup fer the watch?"

"Both or none," I said, looking the old man straight in the eye. "This is a good watch, and it keeps perfect time, too," I told him.

"You drive a hard bargain, Sonny, but yuh gotta deal."

So Old Man Hansen took the watch and I had me two redbone hound pups. Was I ever proud of myself.

I rode down the shell rock drive along the pasture, the pups bouncing up and down in my bicycle basket. I passed the LaRue house, turned the corner at Main Street, and almost didn't see James LaRue standing there under a palm tree.

"Hey Elephant Ears," he called. "Where did you get them pups?"

I felt my heart pound in my chest. "None of your business!" I shouted back and pedaled harder. He was two years older than I, big for his age, and mean. "Rot scum!" I shouted as I passed, pedaling my bike like it was a locomotive.

When I got to our yard, I didn't see anyone from my family around. I went to the garage where I found a big crate for the pups, and then I sat with them and talked to them like I was expecting them to answer back. "One of you guys is for Daddy," I said. "He works hard at his road construction business and never has much time on his hands. But he once said if he had a good hound, he might just take to huntin'. He'll be happy to have one of you."

The pups nipped at my hands and pawed at my shirt. A couple of our cats meandered around, and our dog, Mitzi, had to sniff both pups before she was satisfied. Then my ten-year-old sister, Angie, appeared at the garage door.

"Hey, Fritz. Lindy made it!" She came up and plopped beside me. "Where'd you get those? Hey little fellows. You're real cute. Sure are."

"Got them from Old Man Hansen," I said.

Angie picked up the smallest one, kissed it and snuggled it next to her face.

"What was that about Old Man Hansen?" came the voice of Renato from the garage door.

"He gave Fritz two puppies," shouted Angie.

Renato looked at them, then at me. He laughed then made a strange face. "Never knew the old guy to be so generous. C'mon Little Brother," he said, forgetting the pups. "Get on out here and pitch me a few before supper."

Renato was the best hitter in the county, and maybe all of Florida. I guess I got to be a good pitcher because he was always after me to pitch to him. Angie did the catching, and she always got to run after the ball in the outfield. Over and over she'd dash off, her straight, bobbed hair bouncing around her face. That day we played until Daddy came home, when Angie ran up and grabbed him by the arm and pulled him into the garage.

"Nice puppies!" Daddy said to me as he came back into the yard. "I'm surprised Mr. Hansen gave them away. You be sure and do something nice for him."

"One's yours," I told him, trying to ignore the uneasy feeling that was starting to settle in my stomach. "So we can go huntin' together."

"Won't that be a fine thing," he said, then went to the pump and washed his hands and face. "You remember this day, children. It will be in history books. That *giovanotto*, Charles Lindbergh, flying across the ocean, solo. What a lucky fellow. Wish I could fly a plane someday myself."

Daddy dried his face on a towel hanging next to the pump, and I wondered if he really cared at all to have a hunting dog or to go hunting with me, his second son. He took one of his whiskey bottles from under the back porch steps. "For celebration." He winked. "For that *giovanotto.*"

Daddy didn't worry that we were in Prohibition and drinking any alcoholic beverage was illegal. Mama always said he needed his *cups*. And anyways, drinking didn't make him mean until the hard times came.

Mama came to the kitchen window and called to us in her soft, Georgia voice. Patient and calm was the way Mama always appeared, but underneath I think she was a bundle of worries. "You children be sure and wash your hands now." I wish I had a nickel for every time she said that.

At supper we took our places at the long dining room table. Two of our chairs were empty, because Grandmother was in Georgia visiting kin, and my oldest sister, Alessandra, was away at college in Jacksonville. Alessandra was smart, and at that time we were considerably well off—rich enough for Daddy and Mama to afford to send her to college and rich enough that we were the second in town to have indoor plumbing.

Everyone at the table was talking about Lindbergh. The twins had toy planes Daddy had given them. My older sister, Felicia, was arguing with Angie about some girl thing, and Renato was talking about going to flying school.

Mama was taking biscuits from the oven, when I heard Daddy ask her where his watch was.

"I don't know Renato. Isn't it on the china cabinet, where you left it this morning?" she asked.

Daddy shook his head. "Quiet! Everyone!" he shouted over the other voices. Everyone stopped and stared. Daddy stood by his chair.

"What has happened to my watch? This morning I put it here on the china cabinet. Tonight it is gone."

He looked around the table at each of us. When he got to me, I looked down at my plate and only hoped he wanted the dogs as much as I originally thought he did.

"Fritz?"

"I know where it is," I confessed, forcing a smile.

"Where, son?"

"I think you'll be glad for what I did with it."

"What you did? Where is the watch!?"

"I-I mean Mr. Hansen gave me a real swell bargain. And I traded the watch for those two, fine pups."

When I looked at Daddy, his eyes were blazing.

"Are you crazy?" he bellowed. I felt everyone's eyes fall on me. Then Daddy was at my side pulling me from my chair, dragging me outside to the porch. "Stpido ragazzo! Io ti voglio picchinare!" He yelled in Italian, like he often did when he was really angry.

I braced myself for a real licking. But Daddy just stood in front of me for a moment, with his hands balled into fists. Then he looked me in the eye and spoke in a soft voice, in plain English. "You go and get that watch, if you want a place to sleep in this house tonight."

It didn't take but a minute for me to gather the pups and start pedaling down the road to Mr. Hansen's. I thought about the supper I didn't get to eat and about how dumb I was, always doing things without thinking them through. Then I had a tight feeling down low in my gut as the thought struck me: *What if Old Man Hansen won't trade back?*

And just when I thought things were as bad as they could get, I heard the squeaking of wheels from another bicycle coming up my rear.

"Hey! Elephant Ears!" It was James LaRue.

I pedaled harder and faster, but he still gained on me. Bang! He kicked my wheel and my bike toppled. I felt a burning pain as my bare leg brushed the pavement, and the pups tumbled from the basket.

"Gotta learn to ride a bike," LaRue yelled, laughing, as he pedaled on down the road.

"You rot scum!" I screamed, shaking my fist at him and holding back the tears. I brushed dirt from my skinned leg, collected the pups, and vowed I'd get even, someday.

The pups were shaking like leaves in the wind, but seemed unhurt. I held them and talked to them a good long while before I put them in the basket and headed to Hansen's house.

Old Man Hansen lived in the middle of a mango orchard in a little stucco house that was crying for a paint job. As I came up his driveway I was hit by the pungent scent of over-ripe mangoes. "Mr. Hansen!" I called.

"Over here, Sonny." He came toward me from deep within the orchard. "Whatcha doin' bring'n them dogs back?"

I leaned my bike against a fence, took a pup in each arm, and faced Mr. Hansen. "Mr. Hansen," I began. "You see…my daddy…he wanted a red bone hound in the worst way, at least I thought he did…but the watch, it belongs to him, and he wants the watch more than the hound pups, not that it's an expensive watch or anything like that, just sentimental." I took a deep breath. "Mr. Hansen, could we trade back? Please?" I begged, looking as pathetic and sad as I could.

He just stared at the pups for long moment, then finally spoke. "I have gotten mighty attached to this here watch. And I ain't got no call fer either dog."

I felt my stomach sink. I tried again. "With such fine pups, you can find someone else to buy them. Please, Mr. Hansen. It's a matter of life or death. Please swap back."

Mr. Hansen scratched his stubbly chin for a moment and looked toward the trees. "I do have to get them mangoes off the trees right soon and haul them to market."

I understood. I didn't hesitate for a moment. "I'll do it for you, Mr. Hansen and—"

He rose his hand. "Done deal." So we swapped again—pups for watch and watch for pups. "Be here at six A.M.," he said.

I'll tell you, I was one relieved boy. It was almost dark when I started out Hansen's drive. "Sonny!" I heard him call. "Come on. Put that bike in the truck, and I'll give you a ride home."

Daddy didn't get over his madness right away, and he had a few extra chores lined up for me to do in the next week. As for Mr. Hansen, he sold one of the pups and kept the other. But when I helped him pick his late-blooming mangoes in August, I did such a good job, he gave me the pup he had kept. I named him Watchdog.

*T*he Turtle River winds its way from far within the cypress *swamps to the inlet, where it moves in and out with the ocean tides. The great ocean was always a part of our lives in Turtle River. We had its sand between our toes and the sound of its surf echoing in our ears. After one stormy night it brought parts of a wrecked ship to our beach, and I thought about the many souls who had been lost in the dark waters of its depths down through time. What secrets do those depths hold? I can't say about that, but I do remember the time I heard the ocean talk to me.*

MONTY
July 4, 1927

Every July fourth our little town of Turtle River had its annual picnic at the beach. On this day, Daddy pulled our truck up next to the thatched pavilion. "The Vicellies are here," shouted Adele Partridge. She grabbed my four-year-old sister, Olga, from the truck and carried her around.

Everyone loved Olga, and called her Little Miss Sunshine, but often I felt her twin, Monty, was ignored. He was the quiet, somber one, the one Mama worried about.

We gathered at the field across the street from the ocean for the main event, the baseball game. No matter how hot the weather (and it was sure to be hot in July), we always looked forward to the game.

That year I was pitcher for our team and Renato was catcher. We had good players, which included the Partridge boys and their sister, Adele, who could hit better than most boys. Before it was over, I had hit two home runs and Renato hit one ball so far out, we never did find it. The best thing about it was that Mama and Daddy were there. The Fourth of July was the one time they saw us play in a real game. Other times Daddy was too busy with his work, and Mama was too much of a homebody to go out.

After the game, we headed for the surf to cool off, while the adults got the food ready and sat under the pavilion. The older girls took turns watching the little children while they played in the sand. I passed Monty playing by himself with his pail and shovel, when a group of us headed down the beach tossing a large ball and racing in and out of the water.

It wasn't long before we smelled the chicken and fish barbecuing on the fire, and we headed back so as not to miss a thing. There were lines of pies: mango, banana, chocolate, and even peach. Ockie Smith's mother made two chocolate cakes, and Mr. Partridge brought fresh cream from his dairy to make ice cream. There was fried okra, crawfish, pickled eggs, mustard greens, root beer and ginger ale. We looked at it all, mouths watering, until someone covered everything to keep both the flies and us away. The chicken still wasn't ready, and the smells were driving us kids crazy.

"Fritz," Daddy called. "How about riding to the ice house with me? We need extra for making ice cream. Donta a worry, they won't be eating without you," he said, reading my thoughts and chuckling through his pipe.

We rattled down the road in the truck to Peters' Store and Ice House and Daddy instructed me on how we could have done better in our ball game earlier. He was not easy to please, and it didn't matter that we won.

Mr. Peters, a big penguin shaped man, was sitting in a chair on the front porch. "Howdy! How's the picnic going?" he asked.

"We need ice," said Daddy. "Why donta you close up this shop and come with us? We are just getting started."

"Well, you know, Mother's been sick, and I hate leavin' her alone," said Mr. Peters, leading us around to the back of his store.

Daddy told Mr. Peters he'd bring him some picnic food. They joked together as we entered the cold icehouse, and each of them grabbed a big block of ice with large scissor-like tongs that were hanging on the wall. They carried the blocks to the truck bed, depositing them next to a big tarp that covered fish nets, buckets, and tackle.

When we returned to the picnic, everyone seemed to be scurrying about like scattered ants. Angie came running to meet us. "Is Monty with ya'll?" she asked, breathlessly. Mama was right behind her with a look of panic when she realized he wasn't.

"How long has he been missing?" asked Daddy. His voice rose and sounded shaky.

Mama was wringing her hands. "We don't know. Angie was with him on the beach earlier, then he wanted to come to the picnic tables where I was, so she let Katie Smith bring him up. I don't know why I-I just didn't see him. Katie left him with Miz Partridge, who was talkin' to him til she saw him headin' over to me." Mama was pacing back and forth. "But I…I never did see him." Her eyes were tearing.

"Everyone fan out," said Mr. Partridge. "We'll find him. Don't worry, Mother."

But just looking at the expressions on Mama's and Daddy's faces made my stomach knot.

Voices called out for Monty in all directions. Some folks headed across the street, over the dune and to the baseball field. Angie and I went to the beach where others were walking up and down, looking, and calling. It made me angry when I saw people just standing, looking in the water. *Why are they looking there?*

"That Angie Vicelli is so irresponsible," I overheard Mrs. LaRue say to her son, James.

Angie was standing next to me and must have heard it too, because she turned and ran away crying. I thought I saw a smirk on James' face. I wanted to punch Mrs. LaRue and James, or at least tell them just what I thought of them, but, instead, I turned away. I walked along the beach, noticed the sun reflecting bright on the sand, but I was in a shell of darkness.

I didn't want to look at the water. I turned away, toward the bank, to a patch of sea oats, hoping to find Monty hiding somewhere in there. He would do something like that—just sit and watch and listen from his own secret place, while everyone looked and called for him.

"Are you here, Monty? If you are, come out. You won't get in trouble. I promise."

I heard something stir and parted the sea oats. I jumped back. A pygmy rattler sat coiled, ready to strike.

My heart was beating in my ear. *What if Monty walked into that?* "Where are you, boy?"

Others were still calling for him. More people were walking the beach, looking toward the surf. It was calm before, but now white capped waves were rushing to the shore. I approached and saw a little shovel washing in and out of the sand. Is that Monty's shovel? A chill swept through me. I heard the ocean whisper.

I have your brother. I have your brother. I saw a little body floating ashore. *He's gone, I have him,* the surf spoke to me. I saw Olga sitting alone, crying for her twin. The ocean laughed at me. *He's mine. He's mine.*

"Fritz! Fritz!" I was startled from a trance by Angie's calling. "They found him!" She pointed to the picnic area.

I could barely feel my feet hit the ground as I ran up the beach. Mr. Peters from the ice house was standing next to Mama, who was holding Monty, crying and kissing him over and over again.

"He must have been under the tarp in the truck, and he climbed out when we went to the back of the store," said Daddy.

Mr. Peters shook his head and smiled. "All I know is, when I went inside, there he was, hidin' on the floor behind the counter, eatin' candy."

Mama scolded and loved Monty at the same time. Everyone breathed a sigh of relief. Then Mr. Partridge's voice boomed over the others. "I'm hungry as a bear. Let's have the Reverend say a quick blessin' and get on with the feast."

And so it was done. The women gave Mr. Peters some food to take back with him, and the rest of us dug in. As you might guess, Mama didn't let Monty or Olga out of her sight for the rest of that day.

I gazed at the ocean and the sun's reflection sparkling on the blue-green waters. I shivered at the thought of the dark depths beneath and thanked God for the warmth and light of the sun, and for Monty, that quiet, headstrong boy.

M *aybe it was my imagination on fire that 4th of July, but on the following October 31 st I had another experience with the sea— one that I cannot to this day explain.*

HALLOWEEN

I was in the kitchen watching Renato and Felicia get their water balloons ready, along with a supply of eggs they had saved—some with a rotten stench.

"Mama!" I pleaded, "I've been expectin' to go with them, and I've been invited to the party afterward at the Partridge's."

"I'm sorry, Frederick," she said, placing popcorn balls on a plate. "You never mentioned anything before tonight about going out with that older crowd. But I believe you are still too young."

I saw Renato look at me. He didn't say anything on my behalf, and I had a sinking feeling. I followed Mama into the living room. "Mama, Felicia's goin'."

"Felicia's two years older than you. Next year you'll be out of grammar school. Then maybe—though Lord knows I don't like any of this mischief making."

"Not a one of them should be a goin'!" Grandmother shrieked from across the room. "The witches and the fairies will be about tonight."

Mama's blue eyes flashed. "Good night! Mother, those are just old wives tales your own mother told you. You said that yourself." Mama turned to me and smiled cheerfully. "Now what kind of costume can you fix for the school party? Angie's upstairs almost ready with hers."

"There ain't any of my friends goin' to that party. I'd rather stay home and read my book of ghost stories."

"If that's what you want, Frederick." Mama sighed and walked away.

Angie appeared at the doorway. She was the perfect flapper girl, in a costume made of sack cloth, decked all over with feathers of every color and size.

The doorbell rang, and Katie Smith came in dressed in a Gypsy costume. Angie squealed. They left the house together, giggling as they started down the street to the school.

Grandmother watched at the window. "They shouldn't be a goin' out there alone," she said. "Not tonight. Tonight is for the fairies and spirits."

"Stop that Mama," said my Mama. "They're just going down the street."

Grandmother shook her head. "And Renato and Felicia? What about them?" she murmured.

I heard a rattle outside and saw from the window it was Sam Partridge in his '23 Ford coming to pick up my older brother and sister. I came up behind Daddy, who was at his desk working in his figure book, and I tried once more. "Daddy, can't I go?" Daddy put his pen on the table, turned around and looked at me.

"Fritz, you have heard your mother. She has the final word about that."

Renato looked at me, shrugged and went out the door. I heard Grandmother murmuring to herself. Halloween always made her nervous, but that night she was like a canary in a panther cage.

Mama went about lighting little candles set in paper jack-o-lanterns in the windows. Olga and Monty oohd and aahd. I grabbed a popcorn ball from the plate Mama had put on the coffee table and went upstairs to my room.

I wasn't going to outwardly disobey my parents, kids just didn't do that back then. But I wasn't going to sit around and listen to Mama and Grandmother either. I plopped on my bed and I munched on the sweet sticky popcorn, while I mused about the unfairness of it all. *All of my friends are out there riding around. I'm the only one whose mother won't let him to go.* I licked my fingers, picked up my book and tried to concentrate on reading. *Why are they treating me like a baby?* I tossed the book on the floor and rolled over in bed. *If I can't go out with the others, then I won't do anything.* I heard Mama come into the room, once, and call my name. I pretended I was asleep and she left.

Finally, I did doze off, only to be awakened by the sound of someone hollering outside my window. It was my brother, with my sister and their friends. "Come on Fritz!" Renato called. "We're goin' to the beach to find turtle eggs. Come on out the window."

Without even a thought, I found myself doing as they said and climbed down the trellis by my window. But by the time I got to the bottom, Renato and the others were in a car and headed down the road without me. Though I yelled to them, they only laughed and waved at me. I hopped on my bike, parked at the end of the walkway, and pedaled as hard as I could. They turned the corner and were out of sight. But I kept on going by the light of a full moon, east on Main Street, across the tracks, down a long stretch and across the bridge over the river. There were no cars on the road.

I took a shortcut and walked my bike through sand under the scrub oaks and palmettos. But when I was nearly there, a mist rolled in, blotting out the moon's light, putting me in darkness. Branches clawed at my arms and legs and I didn't know which way to turn. The air was heavy. I felt a building panic.

Then, just as suddenly as it came, the darkness was gone. The moon re-appeared, and a salty sea breeze touched my face. I could see I was beneath the dune on which the beach road was built. Directly in front of me a large owl was seated on a fence post. Its yellow eyes stared at me before it silently flew into the woods.

I climbed the dune, looked up and down the road for cars. There were none. On the beach shadowy figures were moving in a circle around a light. I crossed the road, crept in closer, and stood behind a sea grape tree to watch. I counted seven figures dressed in dark hooded robes, all small in stature, like children. But I knew they weren't children when they began an eerie chant. *Could they be dwarfs?* There faces were hidden by their hoods. The light—which I now saw was coming from a narrow rod—cast eerie shadows over the sand around the figures.

Suddenly the dancing stopped. One dwarf turned and looked my way, pointing a gnarled finger at me. My feet were like blocks of cement. I wanted to run but was unable to move.

The hooded creatures swooped around me, stared at me with eyes that seemed to glow in the dark. I opened my mouth to scream, but no sound came. I felt myself rise above the ground and float toward the rod of light. Weird sounds filled the air, and I felt I was in a whirlwind. The ocean roared. Just when I thought I was going to lose my mind with fear, everything stopped.

I was standing in the sand next to the rod of light, surrounded by the creatures. I didn't want to look at them, but I couldn't help myself. They had weathered looking skin that was pale and ghostlike.

I thought of Grandmother's fairies and witches. Was she right? The creatures circled around me, wailing and howling. What would they do to me? I trembled, closed my eyes, and prayed they would stop, leave me alone.

They grew quiet. One, who must have been the leader, began to speak to me in my mind and called me by name. I felt a calmness that evaporated my fear. The creature pointed to the ocean. It said, if we people on earth don't change our ways, the animals will one day be gone. The creature bent down and picked up pieces of broken turtle eggs that were scattered about. The wailing began again.

It was shame I felt now, and I covered my face with my hands. I don't know how long I stood there before the wailing stopped. When it did, I looked around, I was alone on the beach—alone except for one large sea turtle. She had come to lay her eggs, and I knew she was the last of her kind. A tear rolled down her face.

I made a move toward her when the mist returned and everything was in darkness. That's the last thing I remembered before I awakened in my bedroom. It was morning, and I had a terrible headache. I saw Renato in his bed next to mine. I reached over and shook him awake.

"Renny,"

"What?" he asked, sleepily.

"Were ya'll at the beach last night?"

"Uh huh."

"Did ya'll see them?"

"See what?" Renato rolled over on his back.

"Why didn't ya'll wait for me?" I asked.

"What are you talkin' about?"

"When ya'll came by to get me. You said climb out the window and then, when I did, ya'll took off."

Renato sat up in bed. "Are you crazy? We never came back by here to get you. And why would I be telling you to climb out the window? You must have been dreamin'."

"Yeah. I reckon." I laid back in bed. My head throbbed, but I felt relieved. It had only been, after all, a dream. I rolled over—felt something scratchy. When I pulled back the sheets, I saw sand and pieces of turtle shell in my bed and on my legs. I felt a tingling go through my body. None of that was there when I first got into bed last night! A dream? I wonder to this day.

Grandmother was with us for another Halloween, but she never again spoke of fairies or witches. And I never had the desire to go near the beach on Halloween night again.

$\mathbf{T}$*he memory of that Halloween night dream haunted me for a long time. But a few months later, just after I turned thirteen, my mind was possessed by another kind of dream.*

THE PREACHER'S DAUGHTER

On one particular Sunday morning, I came out the front door of my house feeling a mite uncomfortable because my dress shoes pinched my feet, and my wool dress pants made my legs itch. My good friend, Ockie, moseyed up the walkway to meet me. He had wavy blond hair, a freckled pug nose, and he was almost the biggest and the clumsiest kid in the eighth grade. The biggest was one of the five girls, and I was the only other boy.

"Say Fritz, you see the new preacher's daughter yet?" he asked.

"No," I answered. Oh, I'd seen her alright—though she didn't see me—and I didn't feel like talking to Ockie about the impression she made on me. How could I tell him it was love at first sight?

"She's a real beaut," Ockie said. He smiled and rolled his eyes. "Too bad Renny's away at boarding school. She's the same age as him."

"Too bad," I repeated, as I bent over to adjust my shoe lace.

Ockie and I kicked a can back and forth in the street as we headed for the church, and on the way we stole a look or two at the small white house that was the parsonage. Except for a big orange cat that stared back at us from the front window, we saw no one around.

When we heard the organ music coming from the church, we knew it was time to get on down there. Ockie's father, our Sunday School teacher, was waiting for us under a tree on the other side of the building. He sat in a chair and we sat in a circle around him on the grass. There weren't fire ants around back then to worry about, like we have today, only mosquitoes and sand flies.

I remember that morning well. Mr. Smith talked about David and Goliath, and then about Babe Ruth and baseball. He always mixed a little baseball with his religion—that's what I liked about Mr. Smith.

After Sunday School I sat in church with Felicia, Angie and Grandmother. Reverend Bradberry, a fat, jolly sort, was at the pulpit. I remember nothing of what he said in his sermon, as I was busy looking around for his daughter, until Grandmother pinched me and told me to be still. But finally I got a glimpse of her way up in the front, hidden behind two ladies with big hats.

After the last hymn was sung, I trailed behind Grandmother and my sisters to the door where the reverend stood with his wife, and beside her was their daughter.

"I must thank you Miz Barlow," he said, "for that wonderful lemon pie you sent over with Angie and Felicia. It was most delicious."

"My pleasure to make it for ya'll," said Grandmother.

I looked beyond to where *she* was talking to Felicia, dressed in blue to match her eyes—blue like the Florida sky.

Grandmother pushed me forward. "This is my grandson, Fritz," she said to the reverend and his wife.

He took my hand in both of his big warm hands. "Fritz, nice to meet yuh." Mrs. Bradberry, the slender blond woman beside him took my hand next, but I was looking beyond her. I caught my breath and my whole insides felt full of butterflies, as I saw those eyes on me.

"Hi, I'm Ruth," she said. She cocked her head and cast a dimpled smile at me. Wispy blond curls peeked from under the brim of her hat. She gazed into my eyes and held out her hand. "Guess we'll be seein' a lot of each other, since we all live so close."

I breathed in a faint scent of roses. I took her hand and mumbled, "I reckon so." My hands felt clammy, and my legs felt too weak to hold me.

I went outside in a daze. Then I saw Ockie talking to James LaRue. LaRue turned his big face my way and looked at me with his little slits of green eyes. "Hi-yuh, Elephant Ears."

"Shut-up, you jerk," I yelled and stepped toward him.

James had gone too far this time, and I was not going to take it. I was pumped up. The muscle returning to my liquid legs, I danced around and put up my fists.

LaRue took a step back, and I heard Grandmother shout. "Fritz!"

I shifted my eyes for a second, and LaRue socked me on the side of my face, knocking me to the ground. I heard Grandmother yelling at him. Next thing I knew I was looking up at Ruth, who leaned over me, looking real concerned.

Before I could get my thoughts together, the reverend was helping me up and Grandmother was making such a fuss, I hurried away, too embarrassed to do or say anything else.

Later, at home in my bedroom, I looked into the mirror that hung over my dresser. My face was black and blue. If it weren't for Grandmother, I would have gotten the first punch. I pushed in my ears and smiled. *Mama says I'm handsome. Does Ruth think so? I don't think I smiled at her.* "Dang!"

Monday afternoon Felicia came flying into the house. "Mama! Reverend and Miz Bradberry and Ruth are comin' to visit us—right now!"

"Oh Lord! Children! Quick! Let's pick up in the parlor."

We shoved books, papers, clothes, an old apple core, and some of the twins' toys into the hall closet. We were supposed to use the living room and reserve the parlor for company, but sometimes we kids didn't. By the time we finished our quick pick up, the Bradberrys were at our front door. Mama greeted them, with us kids hovering behind her. Mrs. Bradberry returned Grandmother's pie plate and raved again about how good the pie was. Mama saw everyone was seated comfortably in the parlor, where Grandmother was already waiting in the fancy wooden rocker.

"I'm sorry Mr. Vicelli isn't home yet," Mama said.

I looked at Ruth across the room from me. She winked at me and sent my heart to fluttering.

"This is a lovely home you have." Mrs. Bradberry said.

"Thank you. We're right pleased with it," said Mama. She appeared so small seated in one of our large overstuffed chairs with Olga on her lap and Monty standing at her side, hugging the chair's arm.

The Reverend and his wife said all the things adults say. "What dear children you have…what a fine October day…nice to see you again, Miz Barlow."

Grandmother sat beside him, nodding and smiling.

"We'd like to invite you and your husband to church next Sunday," the Reverend said to Mama.

I listened anxiously. Though Grandmother was in church every week, Mama and Daddy never went.

"That's right nice of you," Mama said, sweetly. "But my husband is Catholic."

"I understand," said Reverend Bradberry. "But remember, we accept Catholics at our church too, you know. Everyone's welcome."

"I declare. I've told them so, many a time," Grandmother said.

I held my breath, wondering where this was leading and if I was going to be embarrassed again in front of Ruth.

But Mama just ignored Grandmother and answered politely. "Thank you, Reverend for the invitation. I'll tell Mr. Vicelli."

I knew, and I knew Grandmother knew, that Mama would not say a word to Daddy about the invitation. But I breathed a sigh of relief when Grandmother didn't add anymore, and the conversation went to other things.

Ruth and Felicia sat in the corner and talked together. Angie took Olga and Monty to the yard to play. I was content to sit and look at Ruth. A few times she looked at me and smiled, and I felt almost like I was going to pass out.

The next day at school, she smiled at me whenever she saw me, and I thought her smile was like a bright and sunny day. I told Ockie that I liked her and thought she liked me.

Ockie looked at me and frowned. "I think maybe she's too old for you. She's a senior in high school and you're only in the eighth grade."

"So what," I told him. "I'm old for my age."

"You are not! And what makes yuh think she likes you?"

I rolled my eyes heavenward. I knew it was useless to expect Ockie to understand. A person just knows when someone likes him.

Later, when I was home again, I got out the skins of coons I'd trapped. (Trapping was the only way I could get them, since Watchdog turned out to be a pretty sorry coon hunting dog). I nailed my skins to the side of the garage, hoping Ruth would notice my skill if she happened by.

When I saw her coming toward our house with Felicia, I climbed to the garage roof top and did a balancing act I'd been practicing. On the peak of the roof, I was the tightrope artist in the circus.

Felicia stood with her hands on her hips, looking at me sternly. But Ruth smiled and waved. "What yuh doin' up there?" she called.

At the sound of her voice, my heart did a flip-flop and my legs began to wobble. I slipped, then slid down the opposite side of the roof and caught myself on the eaves' trough.

The girls came running around the side. "Are you all right?" called Ruth. My heart was beating a mile a minute, but I just smiled and shrugged.

"Fritz! What do you think you're doing?" yelled Felicia. "You're going to break your neck!"

Despite Felicia, I continued my aerial act for the rest of the week, adding a trick juggling three oranges. Ruth told me she thought I was talented and very daring.

I saw Ruth a lot. She spent a lot of time with Felicia and always talked to me when she was at our house. She was impressed by my homing pigeons, which I kept in a large pen just outside the house, and she liked my pup, Watchdog. She said I had "a way with animals."

One Friday afternoon Ockie came home from school with me planning to spend the night. We sat by the river behind the house and fished.

"Alessandra's home from college this weekend," I said. "She's plannin' a party at our house tonight."

"Swell! We invited?" asked Ockie.

"Nah. It's just Alessandra and her friends. She's lettin' Felicia come though."

Ockie pretended to pout, then he began to cackle when he pulled a little snapper in on his line.

"Hey, we can spy on them," I said. "I've done it plenty of times and never been caught."

"That's the cat's meow!" said Ockie, trying to sound like somebody in the know.

About eight that evening, Susan Partridge was first to arrive with her beau, Herbie Johnson. Mama instructed me and Ockie to stay away from the parlor, and she and Grandmother took Olga and Monty upstairs. Angie was visiting a friend. Ockie and I went into the garage.

We practiced target shooting with my sling shot, played with Watchdog and had a bull session, until the sound of music from the Victrola drifted from the parlor window. We went outside and hid ourselves behind the palmetto trees next to the house, where we looked in the window and saw couples dancing.

We saw Alessandra and Jack swinging their arms and legs back and forth to the rhythm of the Charleston. We saw Felicia and John Perry kissing.

Kissing! Good night! What would Mama say?

Just then, Ockie tapped me on the shoulder and pointed toward the front of the house. "Someone else is comin'."

We watched as two people walked into the parlor. Suddenly I caught my breath and I felt my heart stop. It was Ruth, arm and arm with Jerome LaRue! James's older brother! That high-hat snob!

I felt Ockie grab my shirt. "C'mon Fritz, let's get out a here." And I walked away trying to keep from crying, feeling like I was going to explode.

Ockie went home early the next morning. I guess I wasn't such good company. I just moped around, and after he left I crawled under the house where no one would see me—the way I would often do when I wanted to be alone. There I sat, with the chickens and my dog for company, feeling about as low as low can be. After awhile I heard Alessandra's and Felicia's voices.

"Do you think Ruth likes Jerome?" asked Alessandra.

"I think she might," said Felicia. "She said the strangest thing, though. She said that it's too bad our brother, Fritz, isn't a little older. She said maybe she'll wait for him to grow up."

"That's the silliest thing I've ever heard," said Alessandra.

"Maybe so. But Fritz has a crush on her. You should see him. I thought he was making an idiot of himself, but *she* thinks he's cute."

My sisters went into the house, and I couldn't hear anymore of what they had to say. But I didn't need to. I crawled from under the house and jumped up and down, cheering silently.

Ruth was my first love, and I believed I was going to grow up and rescue her from guys like Jerome LaRue...but Ruth became popular in school, and she went off to college the following year. I really didn't see much of her after that, but I always remembered her.

The demolition crew finally arrived. The new owners had it in mind to replace the house with one of those fancy hotel sized houses that have been going up on the river in recent years.

With so many of us gone from the early days, who would be left to remember, and what will there be to keep the memories alive?

When I lived in the house, Grandmother kept the memories from her time, before any of us were born. Being the storyteller she was, she would listen to me tell of my adventures both real and imagined in the woods and on the river, and I was just as eager to hear her stories of her early years in Ireland. Maybe that's why I was her favorite. For whatever reason, I was the only one who saw the dove.

THE DOVE

I was a couple of hours in the woods with Watchdog that morning. When I returned, Angie and Olga were swinging in the hammock on the back porch. "Did you meet any panthers yet, Fritz?" asked Angie, with a stupid smirk. "Maybe you saw Grandmother's fairies." She laughed. "You're gettin' as bad as she is."

"There are panthers out there," I said. "Leah knows that. She listens to me, too, and believes me."

"Hahh! Leah's just our washwoman. What does she know? Besides she just tries to make you feel good by pretendin' she believes your crazy stories. Olga tells stories too, but she's only four." Olga giggled and climbed out of the hammock.

I felt like punching Angie in her smug little nose, but she was a girl and Daddy always said never hit a girl. So I just told her she didn't know what she was talking about, and she shouldn't go talking disrespectful about Leah.

I headed for the kitchen where Mama was mixing up a batter for oatmeal cookies. As I passed through, I stuck my finger in the bowl and took a mouthful of dough before she could say scat.

"Did you wash your hands before you did that?" she called after me. "Sure," I said (I did, earlier that morning), and I dashed down the hall and up the stairs to my room. I passed by Grandmother's room where I saw her at her desk writing letters. *Grandmother's been doin' an awful lot of letter writing,* I thought.

Later that day my good friend Ockie and I shot baskets with some of the other kids at the school court. Ockie was taller than me, but I could still out shoot him and most of the others, too.

After awhile we headed to my house. I told Ockie I'd show him my fox skins I had ready to send to a mail order company who bought them to use for ladies coats and such. We walked along the road feeling the warm pavement on our bare feet as we passed the church, the parsonage, and the gathering of coconut palms at the edge of our yard.

I took Ockie to the back of the garage where the skins were, and just a little ways from the garage was Grandmother. She was sitting in a wicker chair under a maple tree with the sunlight glimmering through the shadows onto her pearly white hair.

I was noticing she was writing again, when all of a sudden, my eyes caught something fluttering above her head.

"Look at that!" I said to Ockie, pointing toward Grandmother.

"What?" he said.

"That bird! It's a white dove—right over Grandmother's head."

"Stop being goofy, Fritz," he said. "There's no bird there."

Just then Angie came toward us from the house. "Hey, what yuh doin'?" she said.

"Hey, Angie, do you see that dove over Grandmother?" I asked her.

"Where? I don't see a dove," she said.

I turned back toward Grandmother. The dove was gone, and just then Grandmother's head slumped down on her chest, her writing paper fell to her feet. My pigeons cooed in their cage.

We all ran toward Grandmother. We shook her and called to her, but she didn't answer.

"Is she breathing?" Angie asked, frantically.

I shook her again. "Get Mama, quick!" I yelled.

Everything was a blur after that. Somehow we moved Grandmother into the house, Daddy came home, relatives were called and a funeral planned.

I recall Ockie looking at me, his usual pink color gone. "I hope you don't see any dove over my head," he said.

I was alone in the garage, tears running down my cheeks. Something inside was gnawing away at me. *Grandmother was always good to me. She gave me my pigeons.*

"Why did she have to die like that. Why did I see what I saw?"

"You really did see it, didn't you?"

I turned and saw Angie, her dark eyes staring at me. At first I was angry that she overheard me talking to myself, then relieved that she knew the truth. "I saw a white dove. That's what I saw."

Angie hesitated. "Ockie says you saw the Angel of Death."

My mind began to race in all directions. "What if that's true? What if I see it again over someone else?"

"Maybe you oughta talk to a person who knows about such things," Angie said.

"I reckon I oughta. But who?"

"The reverend might."

"No," I snapped. "He wouldn't know." I wasn't going to tell him and take a chance Ruth would find out and think I was crazy.

"How about Leah?" Angie suggested. "Remember she said she had a vision after her husband died. The reverend said that certain people do that."

"You're right. I could talk to Leah."

"She'll be home, it's Saturday. Let's go."

Usually I'd tell Angie to go play with the girls, but this time I was glad for her company. We set off on our bicycles together.

Leah lived across the river and down a long country road. We stopped at Ockie's along the way, and he wanted to go, too.

The three of us pulled our bikes into Leah's driveway. Her small, neat, shingled house was surrounded by shining white sand and tall pine trees, with the river sparkling in the background. Her oldest daughter, Mame, let us in and led us into the tiny living room.

Leah came from the kitchen. She was tall and black, and she wore a red bandanna around her head.

"Why, what yuh young 'uns be doin' here? What brings ya'll to Leah's house? I heard about yuh gram, Fritz and Angie. I's so sorry. She was a good woman, that she was. I'll be at the funeral this afternoon."

"Yes ma'am," I said.

"C'mon in here and let me make ya'll something to drink."

Leah motioned for us to sit at her table, which took up most of the kitchen. The room smelled of lemons. She went about her work, humming a church song.

Over the years I had spent many an hour talking with Leah, as she stood over the big round wooden wash bucket in our backyard, churning the wash with a wooden pole. But now, I just sat chewing on a hangnail and staring at a picture of Jesus on Leah's kitchen wall.

"Fritz saw a white dove a flutterin' around Grandmother's head, just before she died, and no one else could see it," Angie said abruptly.

Leah put the lemonade on the table.

"We thought it might be the Angel of Death he was seein'," said Ockie.

Leah knitted her brows together, then leaned down toward me.

"Since you saw a vision of your husband after he died," I said, "I-I figured you might be able to help me."

"I see. Yuh don't understand what yuh been seein'."

"I saw the dove, and then she died," I said. "Angie and Ockie are the only other people who know about it."

Leah rolled her eyes way back in her head, then looked at me again. "Yuh thinks yuh seen the future. That maybe yuh's to blame. Poor Fritz."

Then Leah shook all over with laughter, scaring the wits out of me.

"Yuh Gram was about to die, and she knowed it, bless her soul. I knowed she been writin' all them letters. She was a sayin' her goodbyes, that she was. What yuh seen was not the Angel of Death, but the Holy Spirit a comin' to carry yuh poor old Gram's soul to Heaven." Leah's tall form rose above us. "Now, go tell yuh Mama about what yuh seen. She be glad to know."

After we left Leah's house I felt as though a heavy weight had dropped from my chest. I was anxious to tell Mama that Grandmother was in heaven.

Just before the funeral service I was in the kitchen alone with Mama. When I told her what I'd seen, she got new tears in her eyes and gave me a hug.

"I declare. Frederick, when you were just a little boy I believed you to be psychic. You seemed to know what I was goin' to say before I said it." She smiled. "But you're not a little boy anymore. Why, you just tower over me."

"Mama, everyone towers over you."

"Son, I believe in what you saw." She wiped her eyes with her apron. "I heard of others who had seen such visions—including Leah. I think this might be one of those times that the Lord Almighty gives one of us a little peek at eternity—just enough to reassure the rest of us. Leah's right. You saw your grandmother's soul being taken to heaven."

That night in my sleep I dreamed about the dove again. It was fluttering over Grandmother's head like before. She was sitting outside in her chair with the blue sky about her. When she saw me looking at her, she held up her index finger and smiled at me. Then she vanished from my dream's eye.

The two men from the wrecking crew walked down to the river. Didn't know what they were waiting for. Maybe they were thinking about coming back with fishing poles. Except fishing is nothing down there compared to how it used to be. Life centered around the river when I was growing up, and I can think of plenty a time when folks turned to it for survival.

EVAN

There was a deep hole down river from us, where the fish would sit in the shadows of sunken logs just waiting to be caught.

One afternoon I had promised Mama I'd get some snaps for supper. I rowed up river in my boat and spotted two big ones. I was getting my gig ready, when I heard the hum of a motorboat behind me. I watched as it got closer and closer. If there was one thing I always wanted back then, it was a motorboat. When it got close I saw it was driven by a boy who I had never seen before. He started circling around like he was trying to scare the fish away.

"Hey!" I yelled and glared at him. *What does he think he's doing. Who does he think he is anyhow?* After a couple of circles he headed down stream and disappeared into the mangroves. I looked into the deep, clear water, and I was furious. The fish were gone! That showoff idiot scared them away. I decided he must belong to the new folks who were moving into the house across the river from us.

Later that evening we sat in the kitchen. The room smelled of Daddy's pipe and kerosene oil Mama was painting on the screens to keep the sand flies out. Summer was not quite here by the calendar, but you wouldn't have known it by the sand flies outside our house.

"Frederick, have you met the Hale boy yet?" Mama asked.

"I reckon I saw him up river this afternoon in a motorboat," I said. "He scared the snapper I was goin' to catch."

"My, if that isn't a grand excuse for us having mullet instead of snapper for supper," said Felicia, who had her hands in the sink finishing up the dishes.

"They're a fine family, so I've heard," Mama went on. "Mr. Hale is an artist and a naturalist of some acclaim, and Miz. Hale, I recall, was once a silent film actress."

"Do they have any girls?" Angie asked from across the room. She was working on some kind of outfit for herself. Ever since Daddy got Mama a sewing machine, Angie started sewing on any kind of material she could find.

"No, dolce, they donta have girls," Daddy answered from his chair in the corner. "Only one child, and he is Fritz's age."

I wondered what it would be like to be the only kid in my family. With seven of us, it was hard for me to imagine. I decided that kid, Evan, must be a spoiled, rich brat.

Just then I heard our dogs barking. Felicia was looking out the window over the sink. "Someone's coming," she said.

Daddy stood up and walked across the room. "I helped the Hales move in this afternoon. I told them to come here tonight."

Mama looked astonished. "Good night, Renato! Why didn't you tell me? I'd have made extra dessert."

"Donta worry mama. Take out the soda crackers and I'll get some whiskey from under the steps."

"Renato, you hardly know them!" she whispered.

"I know them well enough," said Daddy. And he opened the door.

Mr. Hale nodded and stepped into the kitchen with his boy behind him. Mr. Hale was a sight to behold. He had a long black beard and long black hair. His skin was like leather, and his eyes were yellow green. He wore a fancy jacket, like the Seminoles wear, and had moccasins on his feet. Daddy introduced Mama to Mr. Hale and his son, Evan.

"Howdy," said the older Hale.

Evan came out from behind his father. He was about my height, had a round freckled face and grey eyes. He was wearing a pair of blue britches and a white shirt. Smiling slightly, he kept his eyes on his moccasined feet that didn't seem to fit with the rest of his appearance.

"It's mighty nice to meet ya'll," said Mama, reaching out her hand. "These are our children, Frederick, Felicia, and Angelina. Our two young ones are in bed, and our two oldest are away from home."

"Where is Mrs. Hale?" asked Daddy.

"Sasha doesn't like coming out in the night air."

Mr. Hale pulled a bottle from a sack he was holding and handed it to Daddy. "This is for your help this afternoon."

"Thank you," said Daddy. He read the label. "From England. You must have connections. This is top of the line."

Mr. Hale nodded, and Daddy quickly pulled a chair back for him and another one for Evan. "Sit, please," he said. "Mary, get root beer for the children."

"Mighty pretty girls there, Renato. Mind if I sketch them?"

Daddy smiled and gestured an approval with his hands. Mr. Hale pulled paper and a packet of charcoal from his sack.

Angie and Felicia's dark eyes beamed. The girls would treasure their sketches forever.

Evan sat by his daddy and didn't say a word, nor did he look at anyone directly. I could tell that this kid was going to be a dull bore. At least his daddy was interesting.

"Fritz, show Evan around," Daddy said. "Maybe he'd like to see your animals."

"Evan *would* like that," said Mr. Hale.

Mama was immediately upon us with the citronella. "Boys. Ya'll better put some of this on. The sun is going down and the sand flies and mosquitoes will be bad out there."

After we splashed on the citronella, I signaled Evan to follow me, and we headed out the door.

"Show him the homing pigeons," Daddy called to me.

I shrugged and wished I could stay there and listen to what Mr. Hale had to say. But I headed toward the large pen with Evan behind me. The pigeons cooed softly as we came near.

"Where'd yuh get them?" asked Evan, speaking for the first time.

"My grandmother gave them to me for my last birthday. She ordered them from up in Connecticut," I said, then opened the door and led him into the pen. "They were just babies when I got them." I picked up one and handed it to Evan.

"Will they fly away if you let them out?" he asked. He stroked its feathers.

"They'll fly out, but they won't go anyplace." I said. "Once we took them to Miami and let them loose."

"What happened?"

"They were waitin' for us when we returned home. That's why they're called homin' pigeons."

"Oh, of course," said Evan.

I just rolled my eyes and didn't say anymore. We left the cage and walked down by the river, where the mullet were dancing in the water, giving us a noisy show. A breeze picked up and kept the bugs away.

"Nice motorboat you have," I said.

"Would you like to ride in it tomorrow?"

A ride in his motorboat. Not like havin' my own boat, I thought, but answered, "Sure," careful not to sound to eager.

"You got fine places around here to go," said Evan.

I climbed the oak tree, at the river's edge, to a wide branch. He followed and we sat quiet for a minute. I looked to the east and could see the beam from the lighthouse by the inlet.

"What's your school like," he asked.

"Good as far as schools go, I reckon. You gottta meet Ockie. He's my best friend." After saying that, I wondered if I was ready to share Ockie with him.

"You like baseball?" I asked.

I stood up and climbed higher in the tree. Evan got more talkative and told me of the baseball games he saw with his pop. Pretty soon I was talking about how I was going to be a real baseball player someday—a pitcher.

I climbed down from the high branch and jumped to the ground. "Race you to the house," I said.

Evan jumped down and I counted to three. I bounded ahead and left him in my tracks. I was the fastest runner in the school. I could even beat the older guys.

We sat on the porch step and caught our breath. We could hear our daddies talking inside. His pop had a loud laugh.

"Where'd you live before you moved here?" I asked.

"Palm Beach," Evan said. "We had a lot of land there, and a big house, but there was some kind of problem. I don't understand, but we lost it all."

"Times are getting tough," I said. "Sometimes Daddy gets to worrying about things. Then he gets his bottle, sits in the parlor, and takes to the cups, all by himself."

"Yeah. My pop likes his, too. He doesn't drink when he's painting, though. He's going to paint the Seminole."

"You don't say."

"Yeah," said Evan. "He lived in their village a long time ago—before I was born."

Watchdog came around and sniffed Evan, and Evan petted him on his head. "My Pop will be really loaded by the time we leave," he said. "I'll probably have to help him home, maybe even drive the truck."

"Lucky you. Me and Mama will probably have to help Daddy to bed."

I decided Evan wasn't a bad kid and not so boring either. I was even looking forward to introducing him to Ockie at school the next day. I had no idea of the adventures we would share in the near future and the things that were to come to both of us.

Evan *became good friends with Ockie and me, and the three of us had some good times together. But still there was always a part of me that liked to be alone. I roamed the woods alone, trapped and hunted with my sling shot. In that time I did things that even to this day give me a pang of guilt when I remember.*

WHINNY

I had my homing pigeons for just over a year, when one morning I went out to feed them and found the cage door wide open. The pigeons were nowhere in sight. I searched, I called, I listened for their sounds. Nothing.

"My pigeons are gone!" I hollered into the house.

Felicia came out in the yard, munching on a piece of toast. "The cage door was open when I got up early this morning." she said.

"Rot! Why didn't you tell me?"

She shrugged. "Thought you were out there. They don't usually leave anyway."

"Well I hope a fox or a coon didn't get in there when they were roosting."

Mama opened the screen door and looked out. "It might be something just scared them off. They'll surely come back," she said.

I didn't see any sign of a struggle, and I hoped Mama was right. Just then Angie came up behind Mama and out on the porch.

"I saw James LaRue outside our house last night," she said.

"LaRue? That explains it!" I felt a heat rise in the back of my neck.

"Now, let's not go accusing anyone," said Mama.

Angie rolled her eyes. "Mama, you don't know what he's like. He was lookin' for Felicia last night, but I told him she doesn't want to see him, ever."

"Well, that wasn't a very nice thing to say," said Mama.

"He's not a nice person," Felicia said. "He's always picking on Fritz. His brother is okay, but he—"

"I'm goin' over to LaRue's and look around," I interrupted, and I started moving backwards away from my family. "Bet I'll find two homin' pigeons over there." Then I turned and ran, ignoring Mama's call after me.

I crept up a short distance from LaRue's yard and stood behind a tree to watch. I stayed a long time but saw nothing of the pigeons. Several times I went back there, once with Ockie and Evan. That time we found no one home, so we searched around the grounds and looked in the barn, but again, no homing pigeons or evidence to say they had ever been there. Even so, I was sure LaRue had taken them.

A few days later, I confronted him in the school yard during lunch break.

LaRue laughed. "Fritz thinks I took his pigeons. Why would I want to do that?"

"You took them LaRue. I know you did!" I shouted.

"Yeah. My brother saw yuh standin' behind a tree lookin' into our yard one day. Better watch out for Fritz. He's a peepin' Tom."

A sick feeling ran through me. I saw other kids looking at me like I was the guilty one. "He did it," I said. "I know he did it."

I was burned up about it, and made sure everyone knew, but that didn't help one bit for getting my pigeons back. After awhile, even Ockie and Evan started to doubt me. Soon LaRue was acting especially sweet to them, giving them things like candy and even money. I stopped talking about the pigeons. No one believed me, anyhow, even though I knew I was right.

I spent more time alone in the woods near my house, practicing with my sling shot. I hit rabbits and brought them home for dinner. One day I was in the woods with Watchdog, when I spotted a sleeping screech owl sitting about ten feet above me on a branch of a pine tree. I took aim and with one shot the owl fell to the ground. I looked at it lying there, still and unmoving, and I felt a hard lump form in my throat.

I had trapped, hunted, and killed animals before. I had my skins to show for it. But a feeling that it just wasn't right came over me this time. I remembered the story called *Rime of the Ancient Mariner*. We read it in English class. It was about a sailor who had killed a bird called an albatross. He did it for no reason, and because he did, bad things happened to him and the others on the ship.

I pushed those thoughts back the same way I pushed Watchdog back—eager as he was to get to the little thing. I swept it up with one hand and could almost wrap my fingers around it, it was so small. It was alive, but it didn't seem able to move. I would take it home and see if I could make it well again.

Mama was in the yard with the twins when I came in with the owl. Olga and Monty danced around with excitement when they saw it.

"Where did you find that?" Mama asked.

"It fell out of a tree in the woods," I said, avoiding telling her the truth. "It's hurt and can't fly."

Mama took it in her hands. "It's so afraid, poor little thing." She held it down to the twins level. "Don't touch it, now. Just look. What do you have in mind to do with it?" she asked, returning the owl to me.

"I can put it in the pigeons' cage," I said.

"You better take it to Doc Roberts and see what he can do for it first," she said. "Then maybe you can keep it till it gets well."

Ockie went with me to Doc Roberts. The veterinarian looked at me suspiciously from over thick glasses propped on his nose, but didn't say anything. He told me the injury was just superficial and would mend on its own.

The owl made a noise that sounded like a whinny, and I decided that Whinny would be his name. Everyone in school heard about my owl, including James LaRue. He came up as I was talking to my friends in front of the school.

"Heard about your screech owl, Fritz." LaRue laughed. "I know a zoo keeper who might be interested in an owl like that."

I felt like tearing into him. *Is that what you did with my pigeons? Sold them to a zoo? You're not going to touch my owl.*

That night I put a lock on the cage, and I stood outside and looked at Whinny. He stared back at me, eyes glowing in the moonlight. Then he made a mournful cry.

"I didn't mean to hurt you," I said. *But why did I hurt him?* I had a sinking feeling. It was the kind of thing LaRue would do—hurting a creature for no reason. "I'll make it up to you, Whinny, I promise."

Whinny did get better. I kept him in the pigeon cage where he could fly around and told myself he was happy there. He's glad to have someone to feed him and take care of him. That's what I told myself. But I never dared leave the door open, and for the whole time I had him, there was always something in a back corner of my mind trying to speak to me, but I wasn't ready to listen—not yet.

BROTHER OWL

One day, just before summer, Evan, Ockie and I planned a camping trip up river. With Evan's motorboat, we figured we could go further than we'd ever gone before and explore territory unknown to anyone.

Just as the sun was beginning to color the horizon, I dropped my camping gear on our small dock from where I could see Evan's house far across the water.

I heard an osprey's cry pierce the air, I watched the bird dive into the river and bring up a mullet in its talons. As it rose into the sky, there came a shrieking from high above. The osprey dropped the fish, and a magnificent eagle swept down, retrieved it, and carried it into the tall pines. The sky was empty. The osprey's cry sounded in the distance, then Evan's motorboat hummed its way across the river, carrying him and Ockie toward me.

Ockie gestured wildly and pointed to the sky. "Did yuh see that?!" he shouted. No matter how many times we saw that drama, it always gave us the shivers.

"LaRue's going to meet us at the bridge," shouted Evan.

"What!" I felt my stomach sink. I threw my gear into the boat and leaped in, taking the front seat next to Ockie. "Who invited HIM?"

"He heard about us goin'," Ockie said and shrugged helplessly. "He came up to Evan and invited himself."

I shook my head. "That guy's a real jerk! You can bet he'll be trouble." *Besides, I got a score to settle with him.*

"He ain't been so bad lately," said Ockie.

When we stopped for LaRue, he gave me an uncommonly friendly smile as he jumped into the boat. "Hi, Fritz." He said it as if he were the nicest, politist guy you'd ever want to know. I didn't believe it for a minute. I just sat in the front of the boat, my face to the breeze while we sped through the water, trying not to let James LaRue ruin this trip.

Egrets and herons flew in front of us. The painted turtles that gave the river its name jumped from cypress knees and floating logs. Some of what appeared to be floating logs were actually gators. They, too, sank beneath the surface at our approach.

We explored fingers of the river we had never seen before, slowing to an idle as the river narrowed and wound through a tunnel of overhanging trees.

"Let's stop here," called Evan, and he turned off the motor.

The water was still and dark. Ockie checked the depth with an oar and could not touch bottom. LaRue stood up and shook the boat from side to side, pounding his bare chest and making ape calls that echoed through the waterway. Soon Ockie was up too, and LaRue pushed him into the water. Within seconds we were all in the water splashing and carrying on—except for Evan. He rowed the boat to the shore and tied it to a small tree.

One large old oak tree had a branch that hung over the river. I climbed it and dove into the water. The others followed; we took turns at the tree, until LaRue got pushy and took more than his share.

Before long we were hungry. We sprawled out on a mossy bank with our food spread around us. I got out peanut butter and guava jelly sandwiches, Ockie shared bananas and his mother's chocolate cake. We dipped our cups into the river for drink.

LaRue wolfed down the last of the cake, and wiped his mouth on his arm. "Let's play Seminole wars," he said. "Evan and I will be soldiers."

Nobody argued with his idea. It was a game we always played when we were in the woods—a kind of hide and seek. LaRue and Evan counted to one hundred, as Ockie and I went off in search of a place to hide. I walked ahead through the shallow bog between the river and the thick undergrowth on the slope of the bank. We had just gone around a bend, when all of a sudden, SWISH!

A huge gator rushed down the bank, passed inches from my feet and splashed into the dark water.

"Holy Moses!" Ockie shouted.

My heart was pumping so hard I could barely speak.

I heard LaRue and Evan coming through the bog. "What happened?"

"A ten foot gator," I spurted out.

"Nearly ran over Fritz." said Ockie.

"Where is it?" LaRue yelled. Suddenly I saw him waving a 22 pistol.

"What you doin' with that gun?" I asked.

"Yeah," said Ockie. "We don't carry guns when we play this game. The rest of us don't have guns."

"You sissies," said LaRue, looking into the water, which, except for a tell-tale ripple, had swallowed up all trace of the gator. LaRue tucked his gun into his belt. "Do you still want to play this game, or are you too afraid?"

"We ain't afraid," I said. "Start countin'."

I signaled to Ockie, and this time we backtracked to the mossy place where we had picnicked, and we climbed up the embankment as they counted.

We walked across an area dotted with pines and palmettos and decided it would be perfect for setting up a lean-to when we made camp.

We found a trail that snaked through a wall of saw palmettos and crossed a path that led to the river. We knew it to be a gator path and moved on with caution.

After coming out of the palmettos we followed the trail through a pine hammock, until we came to a sudden halt. We couldn't believe what we saw. About thirty feet from us stood a Seminole chickee. We gazed at each other, then approached the square wooden platform, with a post on each corner holding a roof of thatched palm branches. Furs littered the floor. Behind it was a smaller chickee, loaded with fire wood.

We heard the snapping of twigs, and LaRue and Evan came out of the trees. "Well I'll be," said LaRue.

When I looked at LaRue and Evan, I saw someone coming up behind them. The hair on my arms bristled as a dark man with long white hair, dressed in a hide tunic, stepped forward.

It must have been only a matter of seconds, but it seemed like an eternity before anyone spoke. It was Evan who broke the silence, speaking in what I figured must be Seminole. He spoke to the man and the man spoke to him. As he talked I looked at the man, his skin like a dried apple, he looked at least 100. Finally I asked Evan in a whisper what he was saying.

The dark man looked at me. "I Brothah Owl," he said.

I felt myself blush, when I realized the Seminole could speak English.

"I listen to white boy and learn he son of white brothah to Seminole. He welcome in many Seminole camp." Brother Owl stepped up on the platform, crossed to the center and sat on the floor among the furs. He gestured for us to do the same.

We all followed and sat in a circle around him. We watched him pull tobacco from a pouch around his waist and roll a smoke. He lit it and offered it to me. I knew my daddy would have my hide if he found out, but I knew I couldn't insult Brother Owl, so I tried it. It tasted different from the tobacco I'd tried once before, but I didn't really like it either time. Brother Owl motioned for me to pass it around to the others and I did.

"Son of White Brothah say you want camp on rivah," said Brother Owl, puffing deeply on his smoke. "Above where you put boat there good high place to camp. Water good foh many fish."

"We're much obliged, Brother Owl," La Rue said, in a voice that I thought was just a little too sweet.

There was a silence, then the Seminole said, "Brothah Owl welcome guests."

"Are yuh here all alone?" asked Ockie.

"Brothah Owl nevah alone." he said. Then he looked thoughtful and said a few words in Seminole, more to himself than to anyone of us. After that he seemed to go within himself.

Evan got up to leave and the rest of us followed. We stood in the open yard for a moment, whispering to one another.

"What did he say?" Ockie asked Evan.

"He said he has a spirit guide who speaks to him."

"Look at him," said La Rue. "He looks like he's ready for the loony house."

"I think he's in a trance," said Evan.

Suddenly feeling uncomfortable, like we were intruding, I said, "let's go," and no one argued with me.

We set up a lean-to in the place we had passed by earlier—the same place Brother Owl told us about. Ockie got his ax and cut large cypress limbs, which were used as poles. We balanced one pole horizontally on the branches between two low palmetto trees. We leaned other poles at

45 degree angles from the ground to the horizontal pole. We cut and gathered palm fronds and wove them in and out of the 45 degree poles. Finally we had our lean-to, with thatching, much cruder than the thatching on Brother Owl's chickee, but we thought it should keep the rain out.

Evan made the camp fire, which he encircled with shell rock for the frying pan. I noticed LaRue had disappeared when all of the work started.

Before long the smells of coffee brewing and bacon frying filled the air. LaRue came from the river with a string of fish. "Looky what I got," he said tossing them to me. "I caught. Ya'll clean."

I shot a disgusted look his way, but Ockie grabbed the fish. "Come on, lets get goin'," he said. "I'm hungry."

It was near dark by the time we had our dinner. We sat around the crackling fire eating fish and bacon and grits when Brother Owl suddenly appeared in our midst. No one saw or heard him come. He placed a package wrapped in hide on the ground by Evan. "Smoke deer meat," he said. "For all."

Evan opened it. "Thank yuh Brother Owl," he said.

"Yeah, thanks," said Ockie. "Hey, sit here and have some of our food."

Brother Owl sat with us. He looked toward the sky and raised his arms, then he ate in silence. I took some of his meat. It tasted wild and had a strange spicy seasoning I didn't recognize, but I decided I liked it. After awhile he got up, nodded to us and disappeared into the dark.

"Doesn't say much does he?" I said.

"Spooky, if you ask me," LaRue said.

Then, as if in response, there came the deep resonant, Woo. Woo-woo. Woo-woo. And we saw a dark shadow pass over us.

"Holy Moses!" said Ockie. "Look at that!"

We all looked into the black night toward the eerie sound.

"I have a story my pop told me," said Evan. "It's about a Seminole who was banished from his tribe."

"Who cares," said LaRue. He stretched out on the ground and passed gas.

Ockie and I held our noses and told Evan to get on with the story.

"...My Pop said this Seminole was accused of a terrible crime against the tribe, and he was shunned by the tribe. Later his accuser admitted to lyin'."

"Ain't none of them that ain't liars," LaRue interrupted.

"Shut up," I said, and Evan went on.

"The trouble was they couldn't find the man after that. They searched for years and never did find him. It was rumored he lived with white folks, worked on the railroad, then got to drinkin' too much and just wandered off and died. But there was another rumor." Evan stopped and looked at each of us.

"Yeah?" said LaRue.

"There was another rumor that said he wandered around until one day a spirit of an owl came to him and told him to return to the forest alone. It said he would become a brother to the owls and protector of the owls. The owls' spirit would become his spirit."

I felt goose bumps as Evan said those words.

LaRue laughed. "Yeah, and I s'pose you're about to say old Brother Owl is that Indian."

Evan shrugged. "I don't know. That all happened a long time ago."

"But his name is *Brother Owl*," Ockie reminded.

LaRue smirked. "He could have heard the story and decided to take that name for himself."

I said, "I thought Seminoles didn't like owls, saw them as a sign of bad luck."

"You know," said Evan, "There's an ancient Indian legend that says the great horned owl was cast out of heaven and sent to earth to bother man-kind. Now if that Seminole was cast out of his tribe, maybe he and the owl—"

"Horsefeathers!" said LaRue. Those Indians don't know nothin' about heaven and hell. They're all heathen."

We talked and argued until a bolt of thunder and a sudden downpour jolted us from the fire to our lean-to. We watched the sky light up around us. After awhile the rain became a steady, light drizzle, with the drip, drip, drip from the trees. It wasn't exactly dry inside the shelter either. We tried to get comfortable. We slapped at mosquitoes and covered ourselves with citronella and listened to the steady chorus of night creatures. Once we heard a far off scream that sent shivers up our spines. "Panther," I whispered. Even La Rue didn't have anything to say to that. The scream didn't come again, and the night chorus continued. Finally we drifted into a damp sleep.

Dawn was just breaking, and a gator was bellowing somewhere by the river. I looked around and saw LaRue was gone. I crawled from our lean-to and walked toward the river where I saw him coming, carrying his .22 and with an empty sack over his shoulder.

"What are you doing?" I asked suspiciously.

"Just looking around, Elephant Ears," he said.

"You're not going to get to me with that LaRue," I said, gritting my teeth.

He ignored me and started down the path toward Brother Owls' camp.

"Where you going," I asked.

"We need dry firewood," he said, and continued down the path. "That old Indian will give us some."

I followed behind him. "Better watch for gators," I said. He waved his gun over his shoulder, and I wished a gator would get him for sure.

When we got to the chickee, Brother Owl wasn't there. LaRue headed to the back where the woodpile was. That's when we saw it. A great owl fluttered into a clump of trees just ahead of us.

LaRue rushed in front of me to the trees and crawled under a thick covering of vines. Crawling in beside him, I was amazed at what I came upon.

We were in a large cavern-like space, with light coming through an opening high above. In a nest were two great horned owls and one little owlet. I knew a thing or two about owls, and I knew it was late in the season to find an owlet as young as that one. The adults snapped their bills and hissed at us. They raised their feathers and spread their wings and became enormous birds. They stared at us with fierce yellow eyes.

"Come on," I said. "Leave them alone." Then—

CRACK!

"No!" I yelled. Too late. One owl flew out the cavity above, and the other lay motionless. LaRue grabbed the owlet and crawled out backwards. I followed, feeling sickened, I heard the little owlet crying.

LaRue put it in the sack and headed for the path with me right behind him. "You're crazy," I yelled. "What about Brother Owl?"

"That old hoot. I ain't afraid of him." LaRue continued down the path.

"Ya'll, get to the boat!" he yelled, when we passed the campsite. "Gotta git from here, now!"

I followed LaRue down to the water, watched him jump into the boat and pull the cord to start the motor, and I knew what I had to do.

I leaped into the boat and shoved LaRue as hard as I could. He lost his balance and fell into the water, pulling me in with him. He managed to top me and pushed my head beneath the surface. I held my breath and struggled against his weight, afraid for my life.

Suddenly he released me. I came up gasping for air and heard screams that echoed off the tunnel created by the river under the trees.

I rubbed my eyes and saw the dark image of a great horned owl flutter above LaRue. Its talons dug into his forehead, inches from his eyes, and blood trickled down his face. I looked on in horror and heard Ockie and Evan shout from the river bank.

Then I heard another owl call from somewhere nearby, and the owl attacking LaRue left him. I followed it with my eyes and saw it land on the extended upper arm of the old Seminole, who stood behind Ockie and Evan. I looked around for a second owl, but saw none.

Standing waist deep in the water, I remembered the owlet and turned toward the boat. In that instant, I saw LaRue waving his gun at Brother Owl.

I lunged at LaRue and knocked the gun out of his hand. Within seconds the owl was upon him again. LaRue sank into the water, but the owl clung fast to his head. LaRue came up and raised his hands to his face.

"Make it leave," he screamed.

The owl left him as if on a command and returned to the Seminole. LaRue climbed to shore, crying like a baby.

The owlet was softly calling from the boat. I picked it up and took it to the shore, where Brother Owl took it from me before I climbed out.

Brother Owl looked at me with sorrowful eyes I will never forget. The adult owl lifted its wings then flew off in the direction of the nest.

The old Seminole looked at each of us. "Earth be yours," he said. "One day you will answer to Breathmakah, spirit above all spirit. When you see highway in sky, he come. He be judge." After he said those words, Brother Owl turned and followed the trail, never once looking back.

I felt there was something in those words I'd heard before. We headed home, lost in our thoughts—except for LaRue who pouted and cursed.

The next day Mr. Hale and Evan went up the river to see Brother Owl, but he was gone and so were the owls.

That night I went home to my screech owl, Whinny, and opened the cage door. He walked awkwardly out the door. I put him on my arm and held it up. He silently flapped his wings, and he flew high into the night sky then swooped down to the woods beyond our house. He never returned.

Ockie, Evan and I talked about the strange happenings surrounding that camping trip. Ockie swore he saw a second owl when LaRue was being attacked, but Evan said it was Brother Owl who made the call I heard, and there was no second owl. We went back and forth about that many times.

As for James LaRue, he never bothered any of us again. Actually, he seemed to go out of his way to avoid us.

And another thing happened, about a week after that camping trip. My two lost homing pigeons came home.

I *got so wrapped up in memories, I didn't think much about what was happening in the present. The two guys were back from the river and talking to some men in suits. Other folks were showing up too, including a photographer from the local paper. I wondered: Are they going to take the house down or not? With so many people gathered around, it reminded me of the time we had a wedding in the yard.*

THE WEDDING

With all the frenzy and goings on that day, I wished I could be just about anyplace but there.

My sister Alessandra and her beau, Jack Wood, were to get married at four o'clock in the afternoon in our yard overlooking the river. Angie and Felicia would be bridesmaids, and Renato was to be best man.

Trouble was Renato was in Jacksonville. He finished his exams at boarding school and was supposed to have arrived home on the train the night before the wedding, but he sent us a telegram that night saying he would be coming the next morning by car with a friend. An hour before the wedding, he was still not home Alessandra was in the house, a nervous wreck. Daddy had already broken into his liquor that was stored under the porch and was passing it out to early guests. Mama came up to me with a frightening request.

"Frederick," she said, looking up at me, "If Renato doesn't make it, you're going to have to be the best man."

I nearly choked. "Mama! I can't! I wouldn't know how."

"It won't be hard. Now c'mon in the house and we'll go through it. And you can slip into Renato's suit."

I told her no, I wasn't going to do it, but in her own soft way, Mama could be pretty persistent. She made me feel as if she would be shamed until she went to her grave if I didn't do this thing to rescue the wedding.

I got my instructions, got myself attired, then went outside and sat against the trunk of a tree near the reception table, praying that Renato would come quickly. Hidden behind tall ferns, I looked toward the canopied site where the wedding would take place. Rows of chairs were already beginning to fill with early arrivals. I had a sick feeling. *What if I do something wrong?* I pushed the thought from my mind and tried to concentrate on other things. I could see Mama, Leah Mills and her daughter Mame putting the final touches on the table.

Leah was smiling and seemed to be reassuring Mama that everything would work out. Maddie Mills and Angie, both twelve, sat in chairs about six feet in front of me under the shade of the same tree. They didn't know I was there. I rubbed my sweating palms against my pants and listened to them talking together.

"Isn't this exciting, Maddie?" said Angie. "When Mame gets married, do you think it will be this fine?"

"I s'pect it will be even more elegant, and bigger too."

"Will we be invited to come?"

"Sure enough."

Angie straightened her yellow, satin bridesmaid's dress, which she had labored over for weeks. It was short and straight and had a big white bow at the hips. Maddie fanned herself with a fancy yellow fan.

She was in a yellow dress too. I thought it set nice with her smooth dark skin.

Angie turned to her. "Maddie, if you could choose, what would you rather be, colored or white?"

I held my breath. *What a dumb question.* Maddie was quiet for a long moment.

"Why I reckon I'd like bein' white," she finally said. "If I was white, and you were colored, then you and yours might be our servants, instead of us bein' yours."

"I reckon maybe you're right," said Angie.

"My mama said," Maddie went on, "if we get educated and work real hard, someday some of ya'll might be our servants."

Now it was Angie's turn to be silent. She looked at Maddie with her mouth open. "Your mama wouldn't say that! She loves us."

"My mama loves ya'll," said Maddie, "but she don't want us to be servants forever."

"Maddie!" called Leah from the serving table. "Get ovah here and fan this cake to keep the flies off! C'mon girl. You been takin' it easy long enough."

Maddie got up, slowly, and Angie sat watching. "Leah wouldn't say that," Angie muttered to herself.

I pondered the words that were said. *Why are the colored folks always our servants? It's the way it's always been. Maybe it's the way it's meant to be. But maybe not.*

"Frederick!" I was jolted from my thoughts by Mama. "Get your dog! Quick!"

I hurried to the reception table where Watchdog had caused a bit of a ruckus. He had upset a plate of cookies, and had one in his mouth. I grabbed him by the scruff of his neck and pulled him toward the garage.

"Frederick, brush your pants off," Mama said as I passed by her.

I sat on the floor of the garage with Watchdog, wishing the whole wedding event were over and done with.

"Frederick!" I heard Mama's frantic voice at the door. I jumped to my feet. "Your brother's not here yet, and it's already past time. We're going to have to start without him.

Jack Wood, the groom, was standing behind Mama, and she directed us both to the front of the canopy.

Just wait till I get my hands on you, Renny. My heart was pumping up a storm when I stood next to Jack in front of the seated guests. I noticed some were looking at their watches. I had my hand in my pocket, fingering the ring, and I stared ahead of me, trying not to look at any of the guests directly. I could hear Watchdog barking from the garage. Mrs. Smith began playing the piano that had been borrowed from the church for the occasion.

Felicia and Angie walked down the aisle, Felicia dressed in pink, Angie in yellow. Each carried a bouquet of red roses. Moments later Alessandra come down the aisle with her arm in Daddy's. She looked like a princess in a sea of white.

Daddy looked like a real southern gentleman in his three piece suit. But I could see beads of sweat running down his face. Guess he was as hot as I was. Behind them were Olga and Monty, looking like two little dolls. I looked out at the front row and saw Mama, her eyes all teary.

We turned away from the sea of faces to stand before Rev. Bradberry. I kept my fingers on the ring, but I was so nervous, I didn't hear the words come when they were directed at me.

Jack poked me. "The ring," he whispered. I managed to take it from my pocket and hand it to Jack without dropping it, then breathed a sigh of relief. After a few more words from the preacher, he pronounced Jack and Alessandra man and wife. The groom kissed the bride, and the lively music began. I walked out with Angie and Felicia, one on each arm. Then there was the long line of people with which to shake hands before we could get to the food.

I was worried the goodies would be gone before I could get to them. But I didn't have to worry. There was tons of food, and Leah kept Maddie and Mame busy with replenishing it.

Everyone was having a good time. The bride and groom were about to cut the cake when a shiny black coupe pulled into our yard. Renato and a woman with a *wow* figure hopped out.

"Hey ya'll. Hope we're not too late," Renato called.

The reception proceedings stopped as we went to greet them. The young woman had short, frizzy red hair, smiling hazel eyes, and she was covered with freckles.

"I want ya'll to meet the former Miss Fanny Flynn," Renato said, smiling.

Fanny Flynn, I thought. *Miss Flynn, that's right, the English teacher who had tutored Renato so he could get a baseball scholarship.*

Mama and Daddy shook hands with Fanny. "Glad to meet you, Fanny. I certainly appreciate what you've done for Renato," said Mama. "But did I hear Renato say 'former' Fanny Flynn?"

Renato and Fanny laughed, and he put his arm around her waist. "That's right. As of yesterday afternoon, she is the new Miz. Vicelli."

The guests clapped and cheered. Daddy went up and gave Fanny a hug, just before Alessandra did. Mama just stood there and stared at them.

When the cake was finally cut there were two brides and two grooms. Maddie handed me my piece of cake, and I thought of the conversation she and Angie had earlier. I would again think of that conversation years later, when Angie, as a young widow struggling to support three young children with a job as a seamstress, was commissioned to sew clothes for Maddie—who did indeed become a wealthy woman.

O ne of the workers was sitting on the bulldozer, but nothing else was happening. Just a lot of people standing around talking. I finally got myself out of the car and walked over to the yard with everyone else.

"Are they going to take this house down or not?" I asked a fellow standing next to me.

"The Preservation Society got a restraining order," he said. "The workers are waiting to hear from their boss now."

"Well, daggone. The Preservation Society. Maybe this house has a chance after all," I said. "I'll bet even they don't know about the other time the house almost came down."

"You a long time resident," asked the man.

"Spent my growing up years right here in this house and the sur-roundings."

"My name's Tom Willis. I'm a reporter for the Town Crier. "I'd like to hear about that, and get it on tape, if it's okay with you."

"Wouldn't mind a bit, but I don't think I could stand here for long."

Tom laughed. "Look, I have a couple of lawn chairs in my truck. Stay right here."

He came back and set the chairs up in the shade of a maple tree.

"Now, why don't you start with the time the house almost came down." he said, turning on his tape recorder.

SEPTEMBER, 1928

From what I recall, it was a stinking hot September day, right from the beginning. I came into the house that morning dripping in sweat, looking for a cool spot, but the air within the house was as heavy as it was outside.

I thought I was still smelling the breakfast Mama had cooked earlier, but as I passed by our dining room I saw a strange man sitting at the table. He had his back to me—a big scruffy looking man with grey blond hair—who sat alone at the long dinning room table, wolfing down eggs and grits, as if he was afraid someone was going to snatch them from him. I slunk into the parlor, where Felicia was curled up in a chair, reading.

"Who is he?" I asked, nodding toward the dining room.

"Shush. His name is Mr. Olson." Felicia whispered. "He came off the freight train this mornin'. He's out of work and hasn't had anything to eat in two days."

"Why did Mama have to sit him in the dining room like that?"

Felicia looked up from her book and shrugged. "Mama said it wouldn't be right to make him eat in the kitchen."

Just then I heard Daddy's truck come barreling around the corner. He honked as he came to a screeching stop. From the window I saw him swing open the door and leap from the truck.

"Hurricane! Mama! Children! Hurricane!"

Feeling a sudden prickling in my veins, I darted from the room. There had been stories of the Seminoles leaving their villages in droves over the past week. A few had stopped by Evan's house. They said they were leaving because the saw grass was blooming—sure sign of a hurricane, they said.

"News just came over the radio at the naval station," said Daddy. "Where is everybody? Get together!" he ordered.

Mama and the twins came running from the river, where they had been fishing. Daddy looked into the sky. "Report said it gets here this afternoon. Got to pick up all loose machinery and parts—whatever is not tied down, put it in the garage."

"What about my rowboat, my pigeons? My chickens?" I asked.

"Where're the cats? We have to get the kittens." Angie yelled.

"Everything. But the chickens will have to fend for themselves," Daddy said.

Mr. Olson came out into the yard.

"Renato," said Mama. "This is Jed Olson. He's up from Miami looking for work."

"Good. We can use him right now," said Daddy, giving the man a quick glance, then darting away.

"I was in Miami in '26," Mr. Olson said. "It was a bad one—destroyed my house."

Mama's eyes widened, and she hurried the twins into our house. None of us in the family, and very few in Turtle River, had been through a hurricane, but Mama knew enough to get food and emergency supplies ready.

When we got the heavy work done, Daddy sent me over to the Harmons, our elderly neighbors, to tell them to come to our house. Their house was a small bungalow, and Daddy didn't think it would make it through a hurricane. On our radio we heard that folks could go to the new Turtle River High School for shelter.

The Harmons were stubborn. "We've been in this house a long time, raised our children here," said Mr. Harmon, "and we don't intend to let a storm push us out."

"I think this is gonna be worse than just a storm." I said. But, they were not going to listen to me or anyone else. I was afraid for them, but I admired what I saw as bravery. *Maybe they'll make out all right*, I thought.

Angie and I brought the cats, Watchdog and our mutt Mitzi into the house.

"We cannot have all those animals in here," said Daddy. "They should be in the garage."

"No!" We protested.

"They'll be afraid in the garage," cried Angie.

I stood beside Angie expecting a tirade from Daddy, but he just smiled and said, "You take care of them."

When everything that could be done was done, we all sat on the back porch, sheltered from the rain that had begun earlier, and listened to Mr. Olson tell his tale. He sure was unlucky. He once had a job, a home, and a family, then he lost it all.

Mama made coffee, fried up a batch of chicken, and made corn-bread. We ate and listened to Mr. Olson, amidst flashes of lightning and loud thunder booms. He talked about that other hurricane he was in, which sent chills down my spine. Daddy turned the conversation to politics and the economy. That's when Watchdog and I went to my room.

It must have been about two o'clock in the afternoon when it got really dark and started to blow. I closed my bedroom windows, turned on my lamp, and settled down with the book I'd been reading. It wasn't long before the wind picked up and the rain pelted against the south window. Watchdog howled, and I tried to imagine I was in an Arctic blizzard with my dog—like in my book *Call of The Wild*—but that wasn't easy in the still hot air of my room.

I looked out and saw the hazy image of our coconut palms bending to touch the ground, whirling round and round like whirling dervishes. Unrecognizable objects sailed by our house.

BOOM! The lights went out. Watchdog howled. I was running down the steps with Watchdog at my heels, when Daddy called every-one to the kitchen.

Just as I got there—CRASH! The windows in the living room, par-lor and dining room blew in.

In the kitchen, Olga was holding her ears and crying. Monty just stared with wild eyes. The wind blew from the front of the house and we all huddled in the kitchen. We closed the doors that led from the hallway to the living room on one side and the parlor on the other, but we could hear the eerie whistling of the wind from under the front door.

"Is our house going to blow down?" asked Angie.

"Donta you worry, sugar," Daddy said. "Everything will be okay"

I'll always remember how calm Daddy was throughout that storm.

A kerosene lamp on the kitchen table flickered and created ghostlike images around the room that matched a thousand howls outside our walls. We kids covered our ears like Olga and curled up on mattresses spread across our kitchen floor.

As the storm wailed, Felicia and Angie and the twins were in and out of sleep. I sat next to Mama by the back door with Watchdog and Mitzi by our feet and my two cats huddled between us. They were all too scared to move and wanted to be close to us.

Daddy and Mr. Olson took turns leaning against the front door with all the power in them whenever the monster gathered its forces and tried to blow the door through.

Night came, the rain never ceased. It was I who heard the noise outside the kitchen door. It was different from the sounds of the storm—a short, weak knock—again and again. When I heard faint human cries, I opened the door a crack. Mr. and Miz. Harmon clung together on the back porch.

Daddy and Mama ran to help them into our house.

"…gone," Mr. Harmon gasped. "Everything, gone."

They were soaking wet and had cuts over their faces and arms. Mrs. Harmon sobbed into her hands.

Daddy shook his head. "You should have come here like we asked you."

"Hush Renato," said Mama, helping Mrs. Harmon to a mattress.

Everyone was awake now. Mr. Harmon moaned as he sank down next to his wife, then put his arm around her.

We strained to hear him as he began to talk.

"Our house blew down. We crawled…so dark." Mr. Harmon shook his head. "…saw a light…your house."

"A miracle," sobbed Miz. Harmon. Her husband grabbed her hand with his free arm.

It was a while after that when everything got quiet. Even the rain stopped.

"This must be the storm's eye,' said Daddy.

I didn't wait for an explanation. I ran out the back door. The stars lit up the night. Water was everywhere. The river's edge, usually some 400 feet away from our house, was now very close.

I thanked God when I heard the chickens under the house. They were safe as long as the river didn't come any closer. I sloshed through water and chunks of debris to the garage and in the dark found the rabbits and heard the pigeons, all safe but scared too.

I wanted to see first hand what happened to the Harmons house and was crossing through the soggy ground across our yard when suddenly everything became black.

"Fritz, get back here!" I heard Mr. Olson call. "Get back in the house!"

I turned toward his voice and the dim light in the kitchen, heard a roar and felt the wind against my back. I tried to run, saw the flicker of the lantern through the kitchen window, but the wind pushed me so I could barely stand. I don't know how I made it to the house. I just remember being thrown against the steps and a strong arm reaching out to pull me in.

The wind was coming from the opposite side now. Everyone had moved the mattresses into the hallway, away from the windows and the back door. Daddy and Mr. Olsen turned our large oak kitchen table on its side and pulled it against the entrance to the hallway in hopes of making a protective barrier. We heard the kitchen window blow in and suddenly the entire house seemed to lift and fall down again. There was ripping, banging.

The floor was getting wet from water seeping in under the kitchen door. We pushed towels and rags along the table and we all wondered about the river. How high would it rise?

I slept intermittently, the howls outside mixed with my dreams. After what seemed an endless night, I awoke to a gray daylight. The wind had stopped, but it was still raining and there was an inch of water in the hallway.

The table had been moved aside and I crept over the sleeping bodies to get to the back door and thanked the God above that we were all still alive. Mr. Olson was standing at the porch rail looking at the water that came just to the edge of our porch. A musty, fishy stench filled the air. A dead heron lay in the sand among tree branches and other debris washed up by the river. A part of our roof was among a clump of uprooted trees. Shingles from our house were all over the ground. I saw tears in Mr. Olson's eyes and I turned away from him.

I could hear the chickens squawking under our house, and I walked toward a solitary chirping at the far end of our porch. Then I saw it. Huddled against the side of our house, looking up at me with drooping, water-drenched feathers, was the saddest looking baby chick I'd ever seen. I lifted the little thing and examined it. "Where did you come from? We don't have any chicks like you, and neither does anyone else around here."

I showed it to Mr. Olson. "I reckon it blew in with the storm," I said.

Mr. Olson gazed at the chick. "Sometimes," he said, "sometimes there *are* miracles—large and small."

T here was something I did back then that repulses people today. Back then most respectable folks didn't like it either, but law enforcement didn't bother with it that much. They pretty much left it alone.

ROOSTER

There were people who lost everything they had in the hurricane. There were people who even lost their lives. We were among the lucky ones, but still we had a lot of hard work getting our house back to normal. Nothing was ever quite the same again after that hurricane.

Mr. Olson stayed around to help replace the roof and the shingles. When that was done, Mr. Partridge found him a job on the fern farm getting things back in order.

Mr. Partridge gave me a weekend job, and I was glad to have it. With Daddy needing extra cash to pay the bills, and with Evan going off to a private school in Georgia, and Ockie more interested in a girl named Eleanor Finch than me—I was pretty lonely.

When not on the farm, I spent a lot of my spare time shooting baskets at the grammar school basketball court and the rest of my time I spent with the little chick we found after the storm, who I named Lucky. He followed me around like he thought I was his mama. He was too small to stay with the big chickens, so I kept him in a small cage when I wasn't around to watch him. I took him with me for bike rides, first he sat in the basket, then he started riding on the handlebars.

Lucky was smart, for a chicken, and feisty. We played a game, where I'd poke at him with my fingers, and he would come at me with his feathers bristling. Soon the feathers began to turn a dark red-brown color.

One day Daddy was looking at him closely. "Fritz!" this chicken is a game rooster," he said.

A feeling of excitement shot through me as he pointed out the small spurs that were beginning to grow on Lucky's legs.

Before long he was big enough to run with the other chickens, and he became king of the roost. Trouble was, he wanted to be king of the entire yard. Mama was particular prey, so she got to taking a broom with her whenever she went outside. One day he almost attacked Monty.

"That does it!" said Daddy. "He goes!"

"No, wait!" I said. "I'll keep him in the cage. And he's smart. Look!" I got down on my knees and called Lucky to me. He walked over to me as sweet as could be and allowed me to put him in the cage.

Daddy shook his head. "Useless bird. Should go into the pot—but he is too skinny. I don't want to see him in the yard, and cut off those spurs." Daddy said that and turned and walked off.

I put Lucky behind the garage, and Daddy didn't mention him again for a long time after that. He had a lot of other things on his mind and seemed to forget about Lucky.

I started taking Lucky down Main Street and sometimes down River Road. Once, riding by a neighbor's house and seeing no one home, I took Lucky into the chicken yard and introduced him to the other roosters. That's when I found out he was a natural born fighter. After that I started taking him on regular visits to farms. I knew of farmers who were gone on certain days, and that's when Lucky and I appeared.

One afternoon, I had him in our yard when a black fellow I knew, named Ivan, walked down the road next to our house.

"Hey, boy, you got a fine fighter there. Reckon you could bring him on over to Uncle Johnny's this afternoon and see how much he's worth?" Ivan grinned. "Course there's some awful mean roosters over there."

"Sure 'nough," I said. "I think Lucky can take on any one of them."

Like everyone else, I knew about Uncle Johnny's Barbecue and the illegal cock fights. I wasn't supposed to go near there, but at that moment the temptation to show off my rooster and my curiosity, was just too much.

"Bout four o'clock," Ivan said, starting down the road. "And don't forget, the shed ain't there no more. Blew away in the 'cane."

I felt a twinge of excitement later that afternoon riding down Main Street, then on out West River Road past some farms, the Baptist Church, and a narrow row of houses, to a sandy road that led to Uncle Johnny's Barbecue. Even though the shed where Johnny did his barbecuing was gone, the folks—mostly men—still came. He now did his barbecuing out in the open, but the men gathered for their games out back behind the palmettos.

I heard the commotion, parked my bike and walked back carrying Lucky. Ivan came over to me with steel spurs. I caught a few stares when I joined the circle to see why they were all cheering. Lucky stirred in my arms.

"Look at that, won't yuh," Ivan said into my ear.

Two cocks were really at it. Feathers flying, spurs reeling, and the squawking was deafening. In a very short time the ground was covered with spots of red and feathers were everyplace. There was a rooster lying still on the ground while the other strutted victoriously.

It was over. The bets were paid, the ground cleared, and suddenly, all eyes were on me. "This is the fellah I told you 'out," Ivan said.

I stood by the ring. Ivan helped me put the spurs on Lucky's feet. Bets were made, though I would get nothing but the privilege of seeing

Lucky win—if he won. Then I thought, *What if he loses?* He was my pet. I raised him. But, there was no turning back.

The other rooster looked fierce and ready, in a cage in the center. I felt my heart pound, and Lucky squirmed in my arms. He moved his wings and squawked. My hands were shaking when I put him next to the cage and stepped away from the fight area. The door was opened.

It was terrifying. I closed my eyes and didn't open them until the noises stopped. It was Lucky who stood alone in the center.

The men around me laughed and slapped me on the back. That day marked the beginning of Lucky's career. From time to time the location would change, but I was always there. Lucky would sit on the handlebars of my bicycle and crow the whole way over to West River. I was nicknamed 'Rooster' and we both became a legend of sorts. Lucky never lost.

One day Ivan and I were standing in the circle waiting eagerly for Lucky's turn, when I felt someone come up and grab me by the shirt collar. I nearly dropped Lucky. When I turned, I saw Leah Mills standing behind me and Ivan, who she also had in her hold. She pulled the both of us to the road. I could hear the men laughing, and I felt embarrassed and afraid.

"What are yuh two boy's doin' here? What would yuh mamas say to know what yuh been doin'?" Leah shook us both with her long, lean arms.

Leah was a good Christian woman, who rarely lost her temper, but on that day she struck terror in my heart.

"Ivan, yuh get on home." Ivan backed away then took off running. Leah looked at me. "Roostah is it?"

I shook my head and avoided her eyes.

"Yuh daddy is goin' tuh have yuh hide."

"Are you goin' to tell him?" I asked, now searching her face for a trace of sympathy. Leah just shook her head and rolled her eyes saying, "Lawdy, Lawdy, Lawdy. Get on that bike and go on home, and ah don't want tuh hear tell, ever again, 'bout a boy called Roostah."

"Yes Ma'am. I mean, no Ma'am," I said. I put Lucky in the basket and spun of on my bike. He seemed as terrified as I was. He didn't stir.

I never went back to Uncle Johnny's. But Lucky was restless and desired a good fight. He crowed all the time, and Daddy was starting to complain about him again.

One afternoon I put Lucky on my bike, determined to find a fight for him, somewhere. But for a reason I didn't understand, as we turned the corner at the end of our street, Lucky jumped down and onto the sand beside the road.

Suddenly, from out of nowhere, there came a large bulldog. He grabbed Lucky by the throat and shook him violently. I dropped my bike and ran toward the dog. A deep bark come from behind me. The bulldog dropped Lucky and took off, pursued by Watchdog.

Lucky lay lifeless in the sand. He was brought in by the wind to become one of the smartest and toughest game roosters in the county, only to be cruelly killed by a dog I had never seen before. No one ever knew where that dog had come from, or where it went afterwards.

I sat and held my rooster. Watchdog came and licked me on the face and sat beside me. "He was only a rooster, after all," I said, tears running down my cheeks. Then I heard an owl call, and I knew it was calling to me.

S omehow Daddy did hear about the things I did with Lucky, and he was hopping mad. I mean he let me know how dumb I was and how a proper boy wouldn't do those things. He told me how a person's reputation is important and how children reflect on their parents and that he was having a difficult time getting work as it was.

DESTINY

One Sunday afternoon I was shooting baskets and dribbling by myself, when Ockie came along dressed in his Sunday best. He came onto the court and put up his hands for me to pass him the ball. I tossed it to him and went after him as he dribbled across the court. I stole the ball from him right under the net and made a perfect shot. At the same moment, Ockie tripped and fell onto the blacktop, tearing his good pants.

"Hey, how about comin' to my house for dinner, Fritz," he said, as he got to his feet again. Good old Ockie. Nothing ever seemed to bother him.

"Your Mama make a chocolate cake?" I asked.

Ockie shrugged. "No. But she has a lemon meringue. But hey, I've missed us doin' things together. I never see yuh anymore."

"Yeah. What about Eleanor?" I asked.

Ockie's face reddened. He smiled, rubbed his nose and bent over to scratch behind his left calf. "Havin' a girlfriend ain't that great," he said. "Besides, she decided she likes John Kirmitt better than me."

I bounced the ball off his shoulder and we both laughed.

I dribbled the ball around the court. "I'm trying for the basketball team." I looked at Ockie. "Wanna try out with me?"

Ockie shrugged. "You know I don't stand much of a chance. Why even try?"

I guess I knew then that Ockie and I would be going our separate ways. Even after Evan came home from boarding school for keeps a couple of weeks later, we were never quite a threesome again.

I was on the court every time I got a chance. Mr. Partridge was our coach, and on the day before the first game he handed me my blue and gold uniform and told me I made it as an extra. I couldn't wait to take it home and show it to Daddy and Mama.

The smell of fried fish and cornbread greeted me when I came in the front door that afternoon. I laid my uniform on the desk by the stairs and entered the dining room. But something was wrong. Everyone was sitting around the table but Daddy, and they were all too quiet.

I felt a tightening in my stomach when I sat down, and I tried to read the expressions in their faces. "Where's Daddy? What's happening?" I asked.

Angie broke the ice. "We have to move," she said. "Next week!"

"What!" I jumped up, knocking the chair over behind me. This couldn't be. "What do you mean we have to move?"

"Frederick, pick up your chair and sit down," said Mama. "You've been gone so much lately, you haven't noticed what's been goin' on around here."

I did as she asked, looking around the table, still unable to believe.

Olga started to cry, saying she didn't want to leave her house. Mama took her to her lap, and then looked at me with her clear blue eyes. "The bank is foreclosing on our mortgage," she said. "Daddy's at the bank right now signing the papers."

I felt really confused and it must have shown on my face.

Felicia filled me in. "It means that the bank is taking our house back. It belongs to them." she said. "Remember Mama and Daddy told us this could happen."

I still couldn't believe it. "So sudden?"

"Not so sudden," said Mama. "The damage to the house from the hurricane set us back. We've been behind on our payments for some time. They haven't been building as many roads lately, so Daddy hasn't had work. He sold the land he invested in over the years for nearly nothing in order to pay off his machinery."

Mama put collards on Monty's and Olga's plates, then she passed them around to the rest of us. "Now let's eat, children. We've a lot to do in the next few days."

"Where are we goin' to live?" I asked.

"Daddy got some work in West Palm Beach with—"

"West Palm Beach? You don't mean we're goin' to live way down there?"

Mama shushed me and put up her hand. "There's a house we can rent right next to Alessandra and Jack."

"It's a small house," whined Angie. "Why can't we live someplace in Turtle River?"

"They're no homes to rent here, and we need to be where Daddy's work is."

I sat at the table, my appetite gone. "I'm playing in the game tomorrow," I said. Then I asked to be excused.

I was in bed before Daddy came home that night, and he was gone before I left for school. I told Ockie and Evan the news when I saw them in the morning. They didn't know what to say to me. Of course by afternoon everyone knew.

That night I sat in the gym before the game, feeling sorry for myself. *I'll probably never play for Turtle River. How would I have a chance at a bigger school in West Palm Beach?*

Then I saw the coach come toward me. He looked me square in the eyes.

"Fritz, I know how you feel. But you got to put your feelings behind you. We need you tonight. Jerry Spensor is out. We think it may be an appendicitis, and his family is rushing him to the hospital right now. You've got to play the whole game, boy!" I couldn't believe it.

The gym was beginning to fill with spectators. I closed my eyes and listened to the echo of many voices and bouncing balls. I was determined to do my best and make this night memorable. I sat alone and concentrated on my moves. The whistle blew, and I was on the court with the others.

Once in the game, I acted on instinct. I knew which way to turn to get the ball, to block the ball, and I knew when to pass and when to shoot. I was small but fast, and I made five shots for our team. We were not expected to win that game, but we beat that other team, 39 to 34. (Our scores were not as high back in those days as they are in the basketball games of the present day, because we had to "jump to the center" and start over each time we made a shot).

The crowd cheered and stomped. We shook hands with the other team. I looked up into the stands and there was Daddy, his fist in the air, he was smiling.

Before I headed home that night, Mr. Partridge came up and talked to me alone. "Fritz, Jess Ross, the assistant coach at Palm Beach High is a friend of mine, and I think, considering how well you did here tonight, he might just have a place for you among his extras."

He smiled and nodded his head. I knew then that though I was leaving Turtle River, I wasn't far from my friends help and support.

It turned out Jerry Spensor didn't have an appendicitis after all and he was able to play for the rest of the season. I was sure glad of that, because I didn't want to have my good luck be someone else's bad luck. Of course I knew I was going to miss Turtle River, no matter what. The place was home for as long as I could remember.

Before we left, the Smith's had us over to their house for a party. There were a lot of our friends and neighbors there. Mrs. Smith made a big chocolate cake for the occasion, and somebody else brought root beer. Friends brought us gifts. Evan, who had inherited his daddy's talent, came with a picture he drew of me, Ockie, and himself standing in front of Brother Owl. Brother Owl stood tall in the center of the picture, with an owl on his shoulder. James LaRue was in the picture too, cowering behind a tree way in the background.

On moving day I was up just before dawn and walked outside alone, except for Watchdog, who stayed at my heels—knowing something out of the ordinary was about to happen. I said good-bye to my chickens and my pigeons. Since we didn't have room for a lot of animals where we were going, a farmer down the street was taking them. Watchdog didn't have to worry though. He would be going along with us, no matter what.

I walked to the river, where the mullet jumped and splashed in the dim morning light. They seemed to bid me farewell, as I looked over the water and thought about the boy I used to be, who freely roamed the river bank and fished its waters, dreaming dreams of other times.

I wondered if I would ever be here again. I turned my head, beckoned by some unknown force. And there it was—perched on a tree branch beside me. The great horned owl. We stared at each other for a long moment, then it silently took to flight, circled and landed on the roof of the brown shingled house that I called home for the first fourteen years of my life. The screen door opened and banged shut as Mama came outside. The owl took to flight again and was gone. An hour later the moving truck came, and then I and my family were gone as well.

I finished telling my story to the reporter. The house was still standing, and the construction crew had moved the heavy equipment away.

"Looks like your house is going to be around awhile," he said.

"Longer than me," I reckon.

"Well," he said, "I enjoyed hearing your stories. Maybe we could get together some other day and you could tell me some more."

"I'd like that young man. But I'm tired now. It's been a long day."

He got my phone number and gave me his card, and I had a feeling I would be hearing from him. There is after all a story to be told.

978-0-595-36049-9
0-595-36049-1

LaVergne, TN USA
18 April 2010
179571LV00003B/36/A